SILENT WOMAN SHOWDOWN

Tom Bantry can't understand why the pretty Cora Lee won't give him the time of day, especially after he rescued her from a man like Rufus Earle. But Tom has other problems to think about. He stands to lose his ranch to the Earle brothers while his friend Silas Sidwell hopes to benefit from the chaos the trouble-makers cause. Ultimately, Cora Lee will have a crucial role to play in bringing things to a head when the time comes . . .

M. C. YOUNG

SILENT WOMAN SHOWDOWN

Complete and Unabridged

LINFORD
Leicester

First published in Great Britain in 2010 by
Robert Hale Limited
London

First Linford Edition
published 2011
by arrangement with
Robert Hale Limited
London

British Library CIP Data

Young, M. C.
    Silent woman showdown. - -
    (Linford western library)
    1. Western stories.
    2. Large type books.
    I. Title II. Series
    823.9'2–dc22

    ISBN 978–1–4448–0765–3

1

Dozing in the saddle, Tom Bantry hadn't been paying attention and didn't notice when his horse turned off the main trail following a set of wagon ruts left since the last rain. Relaxed, the man was resting his chin on his chest putting the dust covered, almost shapeless Stetson in the right position to be whipped off by a long thin branch from a tall leafless bush. Reacting instantly, he came wide awake, his right hand instinctively falling to the butt of his holstered Colt.

'What the hell!' he exclaimed, jerking back on the reins, eyes flashing one way and then the other. Not seeing any sign of danger, he felt the tension go out of his body. Glancing back at the hat lying in the dirt he saw the wagon tracks.

'Damn horse,' he muttered, climbing stiffly out of the saddle.

A tall man, Bantry stood just a tad under six feet in his socks, when he had a pair of socks, and slender. Skinny when a boy, now that he had his full growth his body was wiry and hard muscled, a man more comfortable on the back of a horse than anywhere else. From the worn and floppy Stetson to the high-heeled riding boots on his feet it was obvious this was a cowboy, born and bred.

Bending down to pick up his hat, he stood for long moment, stretching his back muscles. It had been a last-minute decision, not to take the train back home from the county seat at La Platte. Rather than wait another day, he'd decided to hire a horse, a stable animal not smart enough to stay on the trail.

Looking around for some sign of where he was, the man's forehead wrinkled in a deepening frown. Shrugging, the man smiled, letting the frown wrinkles disappear into his more natural smooth sun-darkened skin. He was too young to let a little thing like an ignorant horse ruin his day. Just a couple years past his twentieth birthday, it was part of his very nature not to worry. All over the basin, Tom Bantry was known as an easy-going kind of man.

A happy young man, he couldn't stay angry very long.

'Well, you got us here, you idiot,' he said, scratching the horse on the flat space between its big black eyes, 'so get us out. Which way is quicker, to go back to the trail or go on to wherever that wagon went?'

Not getting an answer, he chuckled and, after settling his hat squarely on his head, swung back into the leather. Touching a heel to the horse's flank he continued on following the wagon ruts.

From the sign left behind, he decided the wagon had passed this way quite recently, possibly even earlier that day. From the depth of the tracks he figured the wagon hadn't been heavily loaded. Likely no more than one, maybe two people being pulled along by a pair of draft horses.

'Probably heading for a hardscrabble spread,' he muttered under his breath. 'Clearly it's a used-up old team of nags not in any hurry to get back to a meager feed box and a lean-to make-shift barn.'

His guess was based on more than the wagon tracks. Raising any kind of beef in this country would be near impossible. High desert was how it was mostly described, a waterless land suitable for straggly juniper trees and sagebrush.

The wagon had wound through the brush then turned sharply to follow the edge of a deep arroyo. At some time in the past, a rush of water pouring out of the mountains he saw in the distance had surged down pushing everything ahead of it, cutting its way through the softer soil. Riding along he reined back when he spotted a stream of dark gray smoke rising in the late afternoon air.

'Looks like we're almost there, horse,' he said softly. 'You'll probably want to stick your nose in a bucket of water, so let's go find out where we are.'

Coming around a clump of juniper, he saw an opening where the brush had been cleared off. A pole fence that had once encircled the half-dozen acres had great gaps in it. He rode through one of the openings.

'Hallo the house,' he called out. 'Anybody home?'

The wagon sat to one side of the house, really a shack, its walls leaning noticeably to one side. From where he pulled up the rider could see the corner of another smaller building farther back.

'What the hell do ya want, stranger?' Someone called from inside the house.

'Well, I'd surely like to water my horse, if you don't mind. And get some directions to the quickest way on into Ferris Corners.'

'The well is over there by the corral. Help yourself.' The man still didn't show himself. 'Get your watering done and then ride on across the yard. There's a trail that'll take you on into the Corners.'

The rider sat for a moment and then kneed his mount ahead. Two sway-backed horses stood listlessly in a pole corral. A long water trough half filled with water stood along one side, a long-handled pump at one end. Climbing down, the man used his hand to clear away the green slime from the top of the water and used the pump to fill the trough. Keeping a watch out of the corner of his eye, he used his left hand to catch water from the pump and drank. There was still no sign of the man in the house.

Taking his time and letting the horse drink, he gave the place a long look. He knew he was being watched and hoped by hesitating the man would show himself. Finally giving up, he pulled the horse away and was about to climb back aboard when he saw movement at the corner of the house. He tensed but saw it wasn't a man shape standing in the shade.

'Hey, damn you,' the loud voice called from inside, 'get back in here.'

'Mister,' a young boy came running from the far corner of the house, 'help us.'

Bantry carefully edged his horse around so it was between him and the house. The boy, running as fast as he could, came around and grabbed the cowboy's leg.

'You got to help us. My sister's in there and . . . and he's going to do something bad. You gotta help us.'

The door of the shack slammed open and a big man came stomping out, waving a long double-barreled shotgun. Stopping, the man stood, his feet spread apart. Big and square-built, Tom didn't think he'd ever seen the man before. The bottom of his face was covered by a long unkempt beard with mustaches hanging down either side of a pair of fat lips.

'Damn you boy, I warned you,' he snarled. 'As for you there, mister, you watered your horse so there ain't no reason at all to stick around. Hear me? You got one chance to get on that horse and ride out. This ain't no business of yourn.'

Tom Bantry stood with the boy holding tight to his leg, staring into the black holes of the rock-steady shotgun.

'Now hold up there, mister,' he called out. 'Be right careful with that scatter gun. I'll ride, but first I have to get this kid to let go of my leg,' he said loud enough for the man to hear, then taking his eyes off the man, looked down at the boy. Dropping his voice, he smiled.

'You just step away, son. Go over there behind that water trough. Go on, now.' The boy, his eyes wide and filled with fear, didn't let go or move.

'Boy,' Bantry said, trying to keep any tension from his face, 'I can't help you if you hang on to me, now can I?'

Looking back at the bearded man, Tom held up his left hand. 'Don't go getting excited,' he called out. 'I'm real willing to do as you say. Nobody ever said Tom Bantry was a fool, especially when looking down the barrels of a 12-gauge.'

Glancing down at the boy's white face he saw tears making tracks down through the cheeks of his little dirty face. Hell, Tom Bantry thought, he can't be more'n ten or so. Facing a shotgun, I'd be scared, too. Bantry almost chuckled, recognizing that the boy was scared.

Tom winked and lifted his chin, motioning for the boy to move. 'Go on now, run like I told you and get down behind that trough.'

Slowly the boy let go and keeping his eyes on the cowboy, stepped backward to duck behind the water trough.

Out of the corner of his eye, Tom saw the bearded man watch as the boy moved away. When the boy dropped out of sight, the bearded man brought the shotgun stock up to his shoulder. At the movement Tom took a step away from his horse and drawing his Colt in a smooth motion, fired as the barrel came level, his slug tearing into the big man's chest. The bearded man fell back, a finger twitching, pulling on both triggers, the pellets scattering harmlessly into the sky over where he'd been standing.

Quickly Tom Bantry ran over and kicked the weapon away. Looking down he saw the man's chest heaving as if he'd just run a mile.

'Sorry about that, partner,' Tom said.

'Damn you,' the man snarled, his voice weak, his breathing not getting any easier.

'Uh-huh. Guess I'd say the same were I lying there on my back like you are. No hard feelings, now. You just lie still for a bit and I'll see about helping you.'

Unseen, the boy came over to stand beside Bantry, looking down at the dying man.

'He was going to do bad things to my sister.' He said calmly, all sign of fear gone. Keeping his eyes on the man lying on his back, the boy spit. 'I hope you die,' he told the man, 'and I hope you go to the same hell my pa is at.'

Tom frowned at the youngster but looked back when he heard the silence. The big man had stopped breathing.

2

Harlan Earle was tired of it but knew there was no way out, he was his brothers' keeper. Had been since they were little kids and except for getting older nothing had changed. Well, maybe this time he'd be carrying enough money that the three of them could start somewhere where people didn't know them.

First though, there was this herd of horses to get over the pass and on up to the buyer waiting in La Platte. At least that damn Sidwell said the buyer was there, waiting. Harlan Earle didn't really trust the man but Stokey did and this was Stokey's deal so that was that. Like it or not Harlan would just have to go along with it.

From when he'd first agreed to join up with Hank Stokey and his little band of hold-up men, Harlan had had the feeling it wasn't going to work out. Look at it, Stokey's reputation wasn't good. Wasn't he known far and wide on the owlhoot trail as Hard Luck Hank? Oh, yeah, they'd made a little money running off cattle from this place or that, but so what? Stealing a half dozen head to sell to the miners over in Ophir wasn't gonna make anybody rich. Not that he wanted to get rich, nobody ever did riding the back trails. But he did want enough to be able to get his brothers somewhere safe.

It'd been a losing battle, trying to keep little Jesse out of things, protect Rufus from himself and at the same time bring in enough cash money to feed and clothe them all. That damn Rufus. He'd sworn he'd never do it again, but like always he couldn't pass it up. Damn him. And taking Jesse with him to talk with Sidwell wasn't a smart thing to do.

'The herd,' Sidwell explained, pointing to a place on the wall map of the basin, 'is in these upper pastures. What you and Hank's boys'll want are there, two dozen of the finest pieces of horseflesh this side of Abilene. To make it even sweeter, there might be another handful of yearlings over this way.'

He hadn't wanted to take Jesse with him but it was certain he couldn't leave the boy in camp with Stokey, Curry and that damn half-breed. No telling what they'd tell his younger brother. He was, Harlan thought, still so young.

Jesse had only been about five or maybe six when the flu had taken their ma and pa. Colonel Ogden Earle, CSA retired went first, his wife a week or so later. That left Jesse, Harlan, the oldest at sixteen or so, and Rufus a year or two younger. For the first few weeks Harlan had found enough food to keep the three of them alive by hanging around the back doors of some of the better restaurants in town.

New Orleans was to be where the colonel was going to make his fortune. He told everyone he'd fought for the Confederacy in the Great War, coming out a full colonel. Harlan wasn't sure, but somewhere along the way he'd begun to doubt anything his pa said. His ma, a gentle woman, never argued with anything her husband claimed.

The three boys lived a precarious existence for the next few years, learning to steal what they could and being fast enough not to get caught. By the time the youngest was going on twelve, they had found an old deserted cabin back in the breaks and what they couldn't get hunting Harlan got by being light-fingered.

Harlan had killed his first man a couple years after his pa died. It'd almost been an accident. The man had returned to his hotel room unexpectedly and found the youngster standing next to the bed with his hands buried in a suitcase.

'What the hell you think you're doing, you little beggar,' the stranger had snarled, pulling at a shiny silver derringer. Luckily for Harlan, the exposed hammer of the tiny two-shot pistol got hung up on the lining of a pocket. Without thinking, the boy flipped open the pocket knife he carried and buried the six-inch blade in the man's chest.

The second man he killed was what sent the Earle boys out of the south. Harlan had only wanted to hit the man hard enough to put him down so he could get at the man's wallet. He got the wallet, but the man was beyond caring. Leaving the dark alley at a run, he crashed head first into another man. Picking himself up, Harlan heard the man shout.

For the next week or so, the three boys huddled out of sight in the breaks. The dead man, it turned out, was a friend of the town marshal. The posse sent out to search for the young killer didn't give up.

Walking, and riding when they could steal a horse or two, Harlan led his brothers north and then when they were able to join a slow plodding wagon train, they went west. The people on the wagon train were Dutch and German farmers going out to Kansas to take up government land under the new federal Homestead Act. Harlan and Rufus paid for their keep by supplying wood and when possible, wild game. The Dutchies, as Harlan called them, didn't know anything about hunting.

They rode with the wagon train for a long time and Harlan was even starting to think he and his brothers might end up working on one of the farms when they got to wherever they were going. That was the first time Rufus went crazy.

It was the daughter of a German couple that did it. The wagon train had stopped to rest the stock and make repairs. Harlan took Rufus and headed out to see about some fresh meat. Jesse stayed around camp, collecting firewood. Harlan didn't think anything about it when Rufus complained and said he was going back to help Jesse. That was good. Rufus was a terrible hunter.

Coming back just a little after dark with the carcasses of two fine bucks tied over the back of a packhorse, Harlan stopped before riding into the firelight. Usually the camp was quiet that time of day with families enjoying their evening meal. This time everybody was in a crowd at the center of the bunched-up wagons. Standing tall in the stirrups, Harlan could see that his brother, Rufus, was standing stiffly at the front of one wagon. A rope had been tied around the upright wagon tongue, the other end looped around the boy's neck. Rufus was standing on a wobbly barrel.

Not knowing what was going on, Harlan knew he had to do something and do it fast. Those square heads were going to hang his brother. Letting go of the packhorse's lead rope, he pulled his rifle and was about to charge in to the crowd but then thought better of it. One rifle against fifty or sixty people wouldn't do any good. It'd only get him killed.

Looking to one side he saw a large

iron pot hanging over a small blazing campfire. Someone's dinner, he thought. Jumping out of the saddle he picked up one of the burning sticks and tossed it into the canvas cover of the wagon. In an instant that wagon and the others he threw burning brands at were ablaze. Back on his horse he grabbed the lead rope and, after cutting the deer carcasses free, circled around, away from the growing fires.

Holding a hand to the side of his mouth, he screamed, 'Fire,' as loud as he could. When the people saw their wagons burning, they forgot all about hanging Rufus and in a wild race ran to fight the fires. That was all Harlan needed. Charging in, he swung his rifle barrel at one man, knocking him down, and came to a halt next to where Rufus was standing on the barrel.

'Here, bend over,' Harlan called. Grabbing the loose rope around his brother's neck, he tore it free. 'Get your ass on that pack horse and let's get out of here.'

In a gallop the two riders fled into the growing darkness.

When the packhorse, an old mare, started faltering, Rufus called out and Harlan turned back. Looking back they could make out the wagon train people fighting to save the burning wagons.

'What the hell was that all about, Rufus?'

'Aw, that old fool, Mueller, he started yelling at me and everybody took it up. I wasn't doing nothing.'

'Rufus, you idiot. You're never doing anything. Tell me, what did Mr Mueller yell at you for?'

'It was that daughter of his, Laisa. The women had gone up that little creek over there to bathe. Laisa was the last one and, well, she screamed and her pa came running at me, calling me names.'

'Did you touch her?'

'Only a little bit. She was standing there in the water and, Harlan, she looked so soft with the water flowing off her long white hair. I only wanted to touch her hair. That's all.'

Harlan groaned. 'That's all, huh? They were going to hang you for touching her hair?'

'I wasn't gonna hurt her. I'd never hurt her, you know that.'

All of a sudden, Harlan remembered Jesse. 'Where's your brother? You were going back to help Jesse get firewood. Where's he?'

'Oh,' Rufus' face blanched. 'I dunno. I didn't see him.'

'I'm right here, Harlan,' Jesse called from the darkness. The two men turned to watch their youngest brother ride out of the night. 'When I heard old man Mueller yell I got out of there. I didn't want anyone to catch me.'

'Where were you, getting firewood?'

Jesse chuckled. 'No, I was in the bushes watching Rufus there. First off I was watching the women then when I spotted Rufus I almost laughed. He was lumbering into the creek after that girl like a crazy bear. You shoulda see it; sure was funny.'

★ ★ ★

The three brothers rode away from the wagon train that night, only going back later to take three horses from the rope corral. Not having any supplies and only the weapons they were carrying, they rode hungry for days.

Over the years since, Harlan rode with different gangs. When they found the run-down cabin in the scrub over on the trail into the basin, Harlan had told Rufus to stay there and he'd go see what was going on. Jesse, now thinking he was a man, wanted to ride with the oldest brother. Harlan was too tired of it all to argue.

Joining up when Hank Stokey came offering a share of whatever they could rustle, Harlan was picked to act as go-between with the banker down in Ferris Corners.

'He won't know you, Earle,' Stokey explained. 'Sidwell wanted me to find someone nobody around here knew and you're it.'

Stokey didn't want Jesse hanging around, saying he was too young and inexperienced. Well, maybe, Harlan argued, but he couldn't just turn his little brother out. So here they were, Stokey and his five men, pushing a herd of the best-looking Appaloosa horses any of them had ever seen up to the waiting buyer.

Harlan wanted the money the horses would bring so he and his brothers could make a new life somewhere else. When he heard a couple of the boys talking about Rufus having won a young woman in a poker game, he knew he had to hurry and get back to that cabin. Rufus wasn't to be trusted.

3

Following the boy to the house, Tom Bantry kicked the door of the shack open, letting the afternoon sunshine in. Everything was a mess inside, fire-blackened pans sat on a small iron stove, a wood table and a couple spindle-looking chairs made up the rest of the furniture. In the gloom he could make out a pole frame bed against the back wall. The boy was working at removing ropes that held a girl down on the rumpled blanket. The girl, he saw, was watching him, not saying a thing.

'Help me, mister,' the boy called. 'I can't untie the knots.'

Using his pocket knife, Tom cut through the pegging strings that bound the girl's wrists and ankles. Glancing up, he saw her unblinking eyes watching.

'Guess your little brother was right.

That fellow out there was up to no good,' he said, trying to make her feel better by smiling. Her expression didn't change.

'What's your name?'

'She's Cora Lee. I'm Bobby Lee. She won't talk, so don't wait for her to tell you anything. I gotta do all the talking for both of us.'

Reaching out to help the girl sit up, she pushed his hand away and swung her legs around and stood up. When she weaved a little unsteadily, he grabbed her arm to keep her from falling. Like a snake striking, her hand came around and using her ragged fingernails, jabbed at his hand.

'Hey, take it easy. I was just trying to help.' Looking into her face he frowned. The side of her face was all bruised, one eye ringed black with broken blood vessels. 'Oh, gawd, girl, you have been treated badly. Look, that's over now. I'll take you and your brother on into town and we'll get you taken care of. There's no reason to be scared any more, you understand?'

'She hears you, mister,' the boy cut in, 'she ain't deaf. She just can't talk.'

That stopped Bantry in his tracks. All he could do was return the girl's cold, emotionless, blue-eyed stare. She wasn't as young as he had first thought, just slender. The dress she wore was long and although spotted by dirt, what had once been bright colors had been washed out and now looked faded gray in the half-light of the room. Her long brown hair hung listlessly. Lowering her head a little and turning it away, the long strands fell straight down covering the signs of the beating she'd been given. He quickly decided the best thing to do was ignore it. If she wanted help, she could ask.

'All right then,' he said, looking away, 'how about this? You get your stuff together and I'll see about saddles for those horses out in the corral. We'll ride on into town, that'd be Ferris Corners. Certainly can't leave you here.' Seeing the boy start to shake his head, he quickly went on. 'Now don't argue with me. You'll be safer in town and from there, well, we can decide what to do next. Now, how about giving me a hand outside, boy, and let your sister collect up what you want to take with us. Come on.'

Not waiting, Bantry turned and strode back into the sunlight.

'The first thing to do is see about the horses. Then we'll pack our friend there inside. We get to town and I'll tell the law about him so someone can come out to bury the body. Let's see if there's a couple saddles in that shed.'

4

Later, after laying the bearded man's body out on the pole bed and making sure the door was firmly secured, the three rode in single file across the open ground. Finding only one saddle, Bobby Lee was riding bareback. His sister, wearing a heavy-looking wool coat over her threadbare dress, sat the saddle like a man, the coat hanging down each side and covering her legs.

While getting ready to ride, Tom Bantry had tried to get the boy talking about his parents but he stayed as mute as his sister. The cowboy decided to leave it up to someone in town to figure out.

The trail was where the man had said it'd be, a faint track winding on south through the trees and brush. Coming up on a little rise an hour or so after leaving the shack, Bantry could see the main wagon road in the distance. Stopping to give the horses a breathing spell, he handed round the canteen he'd filled back at the bearded man's well.

Looking up at the sky, he nodded. 'There's the road down there. I figure we'll be in town in another hour or so.'

Ferris Corners looked the same as it did the morning he'd taken the train north to the county seat. Fact is, as far as Tom Bantry could tell, the little town hadn't changed a bit since he and his pa had first arrived, back when Tom was a boy no older than Bobby Lee.

The town's wide bare dirt street separated the two lines of false-fronted buildings. Behind one row of wood and brick buildings was the Denver and Rio Grande rails; on the other side of this business district was the residential section.

During the hot cloudless days of summer, when the temperatures could easily reach the unbearable mark, the deep wagon-wheel ruts of the main street baked as hard as stone. All it took to soften up, though, was a brief shower. The usual heavy rains of winter, before the temperature dropped below freezing, turned the street into a quagmire.

Riding down the center of the street, the hoofs of the horses of the three riders raised big puffs of dust. It hadn't rained all summer. At the edge of town, where the first building, the feed and seed store, was located Bobby and Cora fell back to ride side by side as close together as the old plow horses would get. Tom had been trying to think of where to take the pair but hadn't come up with an answer. He finally decided the best thing was to head for the deputy sheriff's office.

* * *

Pulling up, Tom turned in the saddle and waited for the two to catch up.

'I think the first thing to do is stop by Buford Sullivan's office. He's our local deputy sheriff and I figure he should hear about that man I shot before someone stumbles across him.'

Bobby Lee frowned. 'We don't need to go telling no lawman anything, do we? I mean, about Cora here and me.'

'He's going to want to know what you were doing at that cabin, that's for sure. I reckon he'll think that man was part of your family and, yeah, I guess we'll have to tell him what we know.' Bantry turned and gigged his horse along, not giving the boy a chance to argue.

Bobby Lee was a feisty little rascal, Bantry decided, wondering how his ma and pa had put up with him.

Tying his horse to the rail in front of the office, Bantry waited until the two climbed down before herding them through the office door.

'Hey, look who's decided to come for a visit,' Sullivan called seeing the young cowboy and coming from around his desk to take Bantry's hand. 'And looks like you brought a couple friends. Now,

30

don't tell me you've caught them darn rustlers that's been causing me heartburn.'

'Nope, 'fraid not. No sir, let me introduce Bobby Lee and his sister, Cora Lee. Bobby is a firebrand kind of guy and his sister doesn't talk much. Cora, Bobby, this here's Buford Sullivan, our connection to the law.'

Neither of the two smiled or took the deputy sheriff's offered hand. Both stood silently, side by side with their hands clasped behind their backs.

Sullivan, a short barrel of a man, stood looking the pair over. Not comfortable in the saddle, when Sullivan had to travel out to one of the ranches he always took one of the buggies from the stable down the other end of town. Not being a rider, he wore flat-heeled, high-topped shoes, which he kept looking good with lamp-black.

'Well, Tom, if nobody's going to start in, I guess it's up to you to explain. You didn't bring these two in here just to stare at me, did you?'

'No. I guess I brought them in 'cause I didn't know what else to do with them.' Pulling an empty chair around, Tom sat down. The brother and sister continued to stand and stare. 'You see, I came across them when the man whose house they were in tried to shoot me. Cora Lee, there, had been tied to the man's bunk and Bobby was yammering at me to help save her. All I wanted was directions and to water my horse.'

The lawman shook his head slowly and, stroking his mustache, walked around the desk to his chair.

'Now that didn't make things much better. Start over. You say a man tried to shoot you. You're here so I reckon he won't be explaining the whys and wherefores.'

Slowly, without any help from the others, Tom Bantry told how he'd come to shoot the big bearded man.

'I never got his name and he didn't have anything in his pockets that helped me.' Turning to glance at the two, he asked, 'Bobby, Cora, did you know who the man was?'

Bobby shook his head. 'He never said,' the youngster mumbled. Cora kept her eyes on the two men.

'We laid him out in his bunk and shut the door to keep the varmints out and rode on down into town. The cabin is about an hour and a half north and a little east of the railroad tracks. We came out of the brush just on the other side of Graves Creek. You'll need a horse to get back up there, though.'

'I'll send someone in the morning,' Sullivan said. 'Now, tell me about these two. Who do they belong to? Where they from?'

'Bobby?' Bantry directed the questions in his direction.

For a time nobody said a word. Eventually, with his head hanging, the boy spoke.

'We haven't had a thing to eat all day.'

Tom had a hard time not laughing out loud. For sure, that Bobby wasn't going to be pushed around.

'Well,' Tom had to agree, 'except for a

handful of dried beef strips I haven't eaten since leaving La Platte. What say we go over to the Mexican's to see what's for supper. Buford, will you come along and join us?'

'You know Mattie's expecting me for supper, but I'll go along and have a cup of coffee. Maybe we can figure things out over there.'

Cora wasn't happy when Tom suggested that Bobby help him take the horses down to the stable. 'You and Buford go along and get us a table,' he'd said over her silent objections. 'Bobby and me'll be along in a few minutes.'

Turning the horses over to the stable hand, explaining that one belonged to the livery up in La Platte and the deputy sheriff would be handling the other two, took only a few minutes.

The Mexican's café was the most popular place to eat in town. The dining room at the hotel was fancier and used mainly by salesmen coming through town and local businessmen. Most of the riders coming in from the range felt more comfortable dragging their spurs across the Mexican's wood floor.

Cora and Bobby made short work of the bowls of beef stew that were put in front of them. Bobby, being a growing boy, was busy getting the last of it, using a big piece of bread to wipe his second bowl clean when Silas Sidwell came into the restaurant. Tom had to smile. He and Silas had grown up together. It had been at the Sidwell home that Tom stayed during the week days so he could attend school. Morton Sidwell, Silas's father, had started the only bank in Ferris Corners. Tom had liked Mr Sidwell and was sad when the old man died.

Strange, some said, that he and Silas Sidwell could be such good friends, Tom all smiles and a willing helping hand and Silas, always looking out only for himself.

Bantry was different in other ways, too. Where Tom grew to be tall and lean, mostly he thought because he did so much work in the saddle, Silas Sidwell, on the other hand, was six inches shorter, rounder and rarely ever was seen sitting on a horse. His place in the world was either on the seat of his buggy or behind the desk of his father's bank. Another difference, one that bothered Sidwell, a fact that his friend never let him forget, was that the banker was going bald. Young Bantry had a head full of thick, black hair, the kind that fell in waves whenever he missed getting a haircut at Curley's Barber Shop.

'Evening Tom, Buford,' Silas nodded and, without being asked, pulled over another chair and sat down. Giving the two young strangers a quick look he ignored them.

'Buford, I've been looking for you. I've some papers over at the bank that I'd like you to deliver for me tomorrow. Legal papers. The bank'll pay for your use of the buggy.'

'Legal papers? Well, I guess that's part of my job. Where do they go?'

'Out to the Davis ranch.'

'Ah, now there's a fine couple, Horace and Lucinda Davis,' Sullivan smiled. 'Tom, have you ever met them? They've got a nice little place over along the east rim. Came into the basin a year or two back, no, more like three years, I'd say, with a half-dozen head of blooded stock, Appaloosas. Davis fenced and cross-fenced a nice meadow and put up a nice snug little soddy. Lucinda and my Mattie have become pretty good friends.'

'Nope,' Tom shook his head. 'Can't say I've met them. I don't get into town much any more, you know. Pa keeps me pretty busy.'

The banker nodded. 'How is your father, Tom? Seems someone said something about him not doing so good.'

'Well, he's not as spry as he used to be. Remember a few years ago when that pinto he liked to ride stepped into a gopher hole and broke its leg? Tossed Pa for a loop, it did, and sprained something in his back. Lately it's been bothering him a lot. He can't get comfortable in the saddle. That means I've just about taken on all the outside work. Fact is, if either of you know of a couple good hands looking for work, I'm about to hire. Got a small herd to make up for shipping.'

Sidwell frowned. 'Seems a little late in the year to be making up a market herd.'

Tom chuckled, looking straight into the banker's eyes. 'Yeah. This one's not a major deal. I'm planning on shipping a hundred head or so. Clean up a few bills before the snow flies.'

Sidwell smiled and stood up. 'You know your business better than I do. I'll stick to banking. Buford, you come by in the morning and pick up those papers, all right?'

'Yeah, I'll be there right after breakfast.'

Sidwell with a little wave turned to leave.

The deputy sheriff snorted as the

banker pushed out the door. 'Boy, he's sure taken over since his pa died. Become quite the mover and shaker, from what I been hearing. You know he fired those two clerks that'd worked in the bank for years and years, didn't you? Went out and hired a couple younger ones. Said he wanted to bring in some new banking methods. I never knew there was more'n one way to run a bank; you put your money in for safe keeping and he loans it out to folk to get them past a rough spot.'

Tom shook his head. 'Like he said, he knows how to run a bank and I don't. Anyhow,' glancing over at the very quiet Bobby and Cora, 'I've got to find some place to bed these two down. Guess a room at the hotel will have to do for tonight.'

'I've been thinking about that,' the deputy sheriff said. 'How about I take them over to Mattie's house? She's got plenty of room and I reckon she'd like the company.'

Smiling at the still-faced Cora,

Buford explained that Mattie was his fiancée. 'We expect to get married just about Christmas time. You'll like her; she's a real nice person.'

'Now that'd be good,' said Tom, relaxing a little. 'I've been trying to figure out what to do about that. Maybe Mattie can learn where their folks are,' he glared at first one and then the other. 'There must be relations somewhere.'

Neither said anything.

5

Victor Garrett knew he was getting close. He figured the four riders he'd been following couldn't be more than an hour ahead of him. Without stopping to look, he was sure the edges of the tracks left by their horses were drying out. They couldn't have passed this point very long before. When gunfire opened up right ahead it caught him unaware.

Swinging quickly out of the saddle, Garrett grabbed his Henry rifle from the saddle scabbard and, ground-hitching his horse, cut into the trees. Keeping near the trail he ran forward.

'Damn it, Butch,' he heard someone ahead call out angrily, 'don't let that fool get away.'

The booming of a rifle and the sound of a horse crashing through the underbrush was the only warning he had when a rider, leaning flat on the animal's neck hurtled past in front of him. When a rifleman stepped out from behind a tree, bringing his long gun down to fire at the rider, Garrett acted instinctively, shooting without aiming. The rifleman dropped without firing.

Another man called out somewhere ahead. 'Hey, Curry, there's someone back there. He got Butch. This ain't worth it, I'm outa here.'

There was another rattle of gunfire and the sound of horses galloping and then everything went silent. Garrett ran forward, stepping over the man he'd shot, another shell levered in the Henry, ready for anything. Coming out of the trees and into a little clearing, he came to a sudden halt, the barrel of his rifle swinging toward movement in the grass across the way.

Holding the front sight tight on the man slowly crawling across the bare dirt trail, Garrett stepped carefully out of the cover of trees. Crouched and ready to duck, he walked over to the man.

'Help me.' The man, hearing someone coming behind him, rose up slightly, turning and raising one hand in supplication. Garrett saw that the front of his wool suit was covered with blood, dirt-soaked blood. 'Don't shoot,' the wounded man pleaded in a weak voice. 'Take the gold but for God's sake don't shoot any more.'

As Garrett bent down, a gush of blood erupted from the chest wound and the man crumpled to the ground.

Scanning the area, his rifle at the ready, Garrett saw another body lying in the dirt a few yards ahead next to a horse lying on its side, its front legs kicking weakly. Walking over, he looked down into the huge frightened eyes of the animal.

'Sorry, old hoss,' he said before putting a bullet between the horse's big, wild eyes.

The dead man lying in the dirt had a pistol near his stiffening fingers. Picking it up, Garrett checked the loads. It hadn't been fired.

'Damn,' he cursed, shoving the six-gun behind his belt. It was clear what had happened. While he had been following Hank Stokey and three men, they had been behind these two. He'd seen one of the dead men before in town. An owner of one of the mines, Garrett remembered someone saying. The other one over there by the dead horse was dressed like a banker, his three-piece black suit setting himself apart from the working-class in the mining district. Once again Garrett knew he'd failed to do his job.

This wasn't the first time, it was just the closest he'd been able to get to the robbers. For some time it had been rumored that Hank Stokey and his gang were behind the killings and robbings. In the past two years half a dozen shipments of gold specie taken out of the Ophir diggings had been hit by Stokey and his men. Somehow it seemed they knew which ones to go after. Garrett, himself a failed miner, had more time on his hands than most others in the area, and had given the matter a lot of thought. He figured there was someone in town, likely one of those men making up the mining committee, getting word to the outlaws. When he had told the committee what he thought, he had been hired to track down the hold-up gang.

'Well,' he said now, his rifle held at his side as he walked back to see about the man he'd killed, 'here's one that won't be taking orders from old Hard Luck Hank Stokey again.'

Turning the dead man over, Garrett looked into the unseeing eyes, trying to remember if he'd ever seen the man before. He hadn't.

A noise coming from the trail brought his rifle up, thumbing back the hammer. A buckskin, its saddle empty, walked hesitantly into the little opening.

'Hell's fire, horse. Maybe you can tell me where the others have gone? No? Didn't think you'd talk. All right, there should be another horse around, unless Stokey and those two took it up. Let's see about getting these bodies back to town. Nothing more we can do here.'

★   ★   ★

Back in Ophir, after turning the bodies of the three men over to the undertaker, Garrett met with the local deputy sheriff. The meeting was held in the saloon.

'Damn it, Garrett, those bastards got off with four sets of saddlebags filled tight with dust and nuggets.' Deputy Sheriff Cosgrove wasn't happy about the incident.

'You'd think some of that gold was yours, Sheriff,' Garrett murmured, taking a sip of beer.

'Well, some of it was, you blamed fool. I thought you was gonna get a handle on them boys. What the hell happened?'

'I was awfully close, but old Stokey had other ideas. Namely relieving those two of the saddlebags they was carrying. Now why in thunder did they think they

46

could slip past that gang?'

'Oh, I tried to talk them out of it, you can believe that. But Fredrick was saying he had to get that specie to the bank in La Platte or his bank'd lose out. I don't understand that and it don't matter. He thought that with you out chasing Stokey and his boys it would be a good time to make a dash over the mountains. So he talked Clairborn into going along. Clairborn's diggings is about played out and he needs more equipment to dig deeper. Fredrick promised his bank would lend him the money if he helped move the bank's gold this morning.'

Garrett shook his head. 'Everyone in town knows Fredrick's bank is in trouble, what with all the lost shipments. He was a fool to think Stokey wouldn't be watching.'

'Yeah. Well, here's something for you to think about. While you were filling out that report I asked for, the miners' committee has voted to up the reward for Hank Stokey. He's worth five

47

thousand dollars now. Dead or alive.'

'Hmm,' Garrett liked the sound of that.

'And something else you likely don't know. There's a rumor going around that someone is out to hire a handful of hardcases. You remember that old man that hangs around the livery?'

'The old coot who tells everyone who'll listen that he once rode with Butch Cassidy and the Sundance Kid?'

'Yeah, that one. Well, it appears he knows enough about those riding the owlhoot trail to get the message. There is money to be made for someone willing to bend the law a bit. Now that old coot, as you called him, swears the hold-up man you shot was talking it up, about how things were getting too tight around here and maybe it was time to move on. I'm thinking if Stokey thinks that way and wants to let things die down a little around here, he might be going to see about this 'bending the law' offer.'

Garrett nodded. 'And who was

making this offer?'

'Don't know. All the old coot could say was that from what he'd heard there was someone up at the county seat doing the talking.'

'Uh-huh. Well, that might be worth a ride up that way.'

'Yeah, especially with that dead or alive reward hanging out there.'

6

It was about mid morning when Tom eventually reached the Flying B. After leaving Bobby and Cora with Buford he'd hired a fresh mount from the livery and ridden for home. Headquarters for the Bantry spread was about twenty miles north of the little town of Ferris Corners and unless a rider wanted to push it, riding well past dark, the practice was to stop for the night near a natural pond. Over the years, an outcrop of boulders had been used, there being some protection from wind or rain with lots of firewood nearby. The livery horse enjoyed a good roll in the dirt before settling down to munch at a small meadow covered with wild grasses.

'Hey, boy,' his father called as Tom came in after leaving the horse in the house corral. 'Me'n Lafe are in the kitchen. You're just in time. I got a fresh pot of coffee. C'mon into the kitchen and tell us about your trip.'

Hanging his gunbelt and Stetson on a hook next to the back door he smiled to himself. Lafe Gunnison had been on the ranch as long as Tom could remember. A man about the same age as his father, he had become just another member of the family.

'Hope there's something left over from your breakfast,' he said, coming into the kitchen and smiling at the two men. 'I had a bowl of stew over at the Mexican's before leaving town but it didn't seem to fill the gap there behind my belt buckle.'

Asa Bantry and Lafe were as different as a rock and a cloud. Where Lafe was weathered, bent and a little shriveled, Tom's father was big, wide-shouldered and robust. The bigger disparity was that Lafe had spent nearly all his life on the back of a horse minding cattle, while Asa was more comfortable taking care of the ranch books. Tom had always thought he got the best of both of them; at sixteen he was a hand that could work cattle but was also able to keep a tally of the stock, out dicker the best of the buyers and keep a set of books that would satisfy any banker.

'So,' Asa said, walking stiffly to the big, black cast-iron wood stove to pick up the blue enameled coffee pot, 'did you get everything taken care of over in La Platte?'

Tom nodded. 'Everything except being able to find a couple or three men to hire. There didn't appear to be anyone willing to come over to the basin for no more'n the couple weeks' work I had to offer. I suppose the likely ones were holding out for a full winter.'

Watching his father fill all three cups, he saw how the older man was holding his back. It was obvious that the pain had gotten worst. Probably be a real bear when cold weather hit, he thought.

'That's the kind of men you find nowadays, all right,' Lafe remarked. 'Ain't like it was when we was younkers, Asa. Back then a man was always looking to make a day's pay, and able to give as good as he got, too, I'll tell ya. Not like today. Buncha fools would rather sit around drinking bust skull whiskey than do a day's work.'

Tom chucked. 'Well, it isn't that bad. I figure they all thought riding down here for a few weeks' work might mean they end up with no chance for work clear to spring. I ran into Silas and Buford in town and asked them to keep an eye out for some likely hands.'

'Humph, that Silas,' Lafe snorted, 'now there's a case for ya. I been hearing things about him since his pa passed on. Seems to think he's the big auger now. Well, I reckon the time will come when he gets cut down to size. Most of them do.'

Asa waved a hand, shaking his head. 'Now Lafe, don't go bad-mouthing young Sidwell. His pa built that bank up from next to nothing and I'm sure his boy learned how to do the job as good. Look at Tom here. Bewtix you and me, we taught him all he needs to know about ranching, didn't we? Well then, I figure old Morton Sidwell did the same.' Looking over the rim of his cup he nodded at Tom. 'I thought you was planning on coming in on tomorrow's train. What happened?'

'Nothing really. I just didn't see any good to my hanging around in La Platte another night so I rented a horse and rode over. I don't know if it was a good idea, though.' Seeing the questions in the two older men's eyes, he quickly explained about the gun battle and bringing Cora and Bobby Lee into town.

'Sullivan gonna go get that man's body tomorrow?' Lafe asked when Tom was finished.

'I don't know. He's got some legal papers to deliver first off. I was more interested in making sure he knew I'd shot the man fair and square before some idiot came riding in and finding it. Bringing in the body, or just burying it out there somewhere is his problem

54

now. Anyhow, he's got that boy and his sister to figure out what to do with.'

Lafe snorted again. 'You shoulda brung them out here. Put the boy to work on the back of a horse and the girl to cleaning and cooking.'

'And what's wrong with my cooking?' Asa Bantry asked. 'The way you put the food away, nobody'd ever guess you didn't think it was the best ever.'

Tom put his cup down and laughing went to the stove. 'Yeah, you two fight it out. I'm going to fry up a mess of eggs and a piece of bacon or two. Lafe, it looks like it'll be up to you and me to start putting together a jag of beeves for the market. Daylight be early enough for you?'

★   ★   ★

Chasing cattle out of the brush was hard work for the two men. It was even harder on their horses. Both had strung along an extra mount when they left the home place with the idea of trading off when one animal tired. By the time the sun was high overhead all four horses were covered with foamy sweat, the muscles on their flanks trembling with fatigue. Tom and Lafe weren't much better off.

'This just isn't going to work, boy,' Lafe said when they took a break for a cup of coffee. The two sat listlessly on either side of the little fire under the black camp coffee pot. Neither had enough energy to tear into the thick sandwiches they left the kitchen with.

'No,' Tom agreed, 'not if we're going to make up this batch with older stuff. They're the smart ones, the critters that know how to get lost back in the thickets. It'll take at least four, maybe five men, I figure.'

Sipping the hot, black brew, the older man sat back on his heels, resting.

'I never did get exactly why you want to make up a market herd. Not this late in the season, anyhow.'

'I had to take out a loan with the bank in town. Not a big one but to keep the interest on the money low, I made it a short term note. Pa and I figured we could pay it off by running a hundred head or so to the rail yards by the first of the month. That's, what, three weeks? Anyhow, by taking the older stuff we'll be leaving mostly yearlings and two-year-old beeves to winter over.'

'Humph, nobody asked me but if they had I'd have argued against having anything to do with that bank in Ferris Corners. I know' — he held up a hand to stop Tom's reaction — 'I know. You and young Sidwell are friends and have been so since you both were wearing short pants. But maybe that's the trouble, you don't see how he's changed since his pa died. I tell you, things ain't like they used to be over at that bank. You ranch owners, you got ways of doing things that us hired hands got no part of, but we hear things. I got a bad feeling about all this, I surely do.'

Tom chuckled softly, emptying the coffee dregs from his cup. 'You old-timers just don't like change, that's what's bothering you. Anyway, that doesn't matter right now. What does is getting a herd made up. Guess I'll have to go back to town and look for hiring some help.'

★   ★   ★

Ferris Corners wasn't a big town, if anyone was counting noses it wouldn't have taken them long. About half of that part of the county's population lived out on the dozen or so ranches in the nearby country that the town served and was known simply as the basin. The Flying B ranch, owned by Tom and his pa, Asa, was the most northern of the ranching operations spread out over the flat country.

As his pa had told the story, he'd heard about Ferris Corners from someone down on the panhandle. That was back when Tom was just a tadpole of a boy. Seems a cattle buyer named Heep had described the area as being good country to raise livestock. Lots of water and good grass all lying in gentle rolling flats across a wide valley that was protected from the harsh winter storms coming out of the cold north on three sides by steep foothills. At that time, Heep had said, not much of it had been homesteaded.

A small feeder rail line, the Denver and Rio Grande, had a right-of-way coming down from the high country to the north, cutting right down the middle of this basin. Typical of this kind of operation, the federal government gave railroad companies huge tracts of land on either side of the right-of-way. That land was then sold off by the rail company to help pay the expenses for putting in and maintaining the line. When Heep had told Asa Bantry about it, there had only been three or four ranching operations in the area and they were all spread out.

The D&RG only ran trains, mostly cattle cars with one or two passenger coaches, in one direction each day. It was the rail line that kept the small town of Ferris Corners alive, that and the half dozen cattle and horse ranches spread across the basin.

After listening to the buyer, who said he was also acting as an agent for the D&RG, Asa Bantry, his wife and young son had come north on the train to look things over. Arriving in Ferris Corners, they had taken rooms at the hotel and Bantry had spent a couple weeks riding around the country, talking to the ranchers and their hands, learning what land was open and where the best year-round water sources were. He'd found what he wanted for his family at the far northern end and set out his stakes over a couple thousand acres, most of them on the gentle slopes of the mountain range at the far edge of the basin. Their closest neighbor was an old man who ran a few head on a series of high meadows even farther to the north.

The Bantrys didn't even know he was up there when they first moved in. It was while Asa Bantry and a few hired men were busy building the house that the old man rode in. The house, a big two-story log structure, sat on a small rise at the base of a steep slope. The elder Bantry was laying cedar shingles on the roof one morning when he saw a horse and rider coming down the slope.

The rider came slowly into the yard and sat on the back of his pinto pony, taking his time to look things over. After being invited to step down he introduced himself as Leander Harvey. Tom, who had been playing in a nearby creek, had never before seen a man wearing buckskin pants and a leather shirt with long fringes hanging down from the sleeves. The boy couldn't take his eyes off the man. When he saw Harvey's horse didn't have a saddle, only a blanket for the rider to sit on, he was speechless.

'Are you an Indian?' he asked nervously.

The old man, his smile showing an almost toothless mouth, seemed pleased at the question. 'Nope, can't say I am, son, although there were times I lived with our redskin brothers. And good times they were, too.'

The story Harvey told over supper that night was one young Tom listened to almost without breathing. Harvey said he'd come west as a young man, trapping beaver. When the beaver ran out, he prospected in California then worked cattle up in Wyoming and even rode shotgun guard for a stage line over in Nevada Territory. Older and looking for a place to settle, he took the little leather sack of gold nuggets he'd once found in a cold, flowing creek up in Oregon and paid for a piece of land to the north of Bantry's range.

'There's a string of meadows up there,' he explained, 'and enough water to keep them green all year round. I raise a few head of horses and enough cattle to pay for what store-bought stuff I need. Up there nobody bothers me and that's the way I like it. Why I don't even believe many people know I'm there.'

Asa Bantry wanted to know how he got his cattle to market.

'There's a high pass on over to the west. I can drive a handful over to the mining camps that way. Them fellas digging up the Mother Earth over there will pay most anything for fresh beef. And they got the gold to do it with, too.'

Tom was sent to bed while the two men continued talking. He was disappointed when discovering the old trapper had ridden off by the time he climbed out of his blankets the next morning. That was only the first of many visits from the old trapper. Over the years, old Harvey would visit the Bantrys a couple times a year, always welcome but never staying more than overnight. When he rode down into the Flying B's front yard a month or so ago he'd been riding a small mustang — the pinto had long been sold off.

The talk that night was different. Harvey wanted to sell his land and what stock was there.

'I'm too old to be running cattle over the pass anymore,' the old trapper said. For the first time Tom noticed how tired the old man looked. 'To tell the truth, I ain't feeling so good. It's time I thought a little about what'll happen when I die. Back when I was living with the Sioux, I remember there was a medicine man who one morning started giving away everything he owned. They'd do that, you know, just up and give it all away, their horses, their weapons and even the buffalo skins used to make their tepees. Usually that'd happen when they thought they had too much and others didn't have enough. Why, these people were the best ones I ever did hear of for taking care of each other. But this time was different. Ya see, he knew he was going to die. Well, I feel the same way. But I ain't gonna give my land away. It's all I got. I want to sell it to you.'

Handing a piece of paper to Asa Bantry, he smiled toothlessly. 'I got a daughter what lives down in Abilene.

She and her husband can likely use the money. Here's how to reach her.'

For the remainder of the evening, the two men negotiated for the land. Neither Asa or his son had ever been up there and had never seen the place so a lot of the talk was the old trapper describing it. He did a fine job, making both Bantry men feel that they'd recognize each of the little pockets of grass when they finally saw them.

Once a price had been agreed to, Harvey simply turned his mustang around and headed back up the slope. It was the wrong time of year for Asa to have that much cash on hand. Finally, after giving the matter a lot of thought, Tom and his father decided to take out a loan from the Ferris Corners bank. That was the money Tom took when he rode over to the Wells Fargo Bank at the county seat, La Platte, to send to the daughter in Abilene.

7

Over the years Ferris Corners hadn't
changed much. Even as more people
came in and took up land the town
didn't seem to grow. Now, as before,
there was everything a rancher or his
wife needed: a feed store that sold all
kinds of stock equipment and the
general store that sold everything else.
A hotel, three saloons, a bank, a church,
and the deputy sheriff's office made up
most of the rest. Tom had been one of
the first students to attend classes when
a school teacher had opened a school in
what had once been a railroad con-
struction building.

Typically in such small places the
local saloon was where someone got
the latest news. The three saloons in
Ferris Corners were the Golden Slipper, Big Gert's and the Past Time. The
Golden Slipper was next to the hotel

and like the hotel restaurant catered mostly to the traveling crowd. Those working for Gertrude Wyatt included half a dozen ladies of one age or another, each with her own room upstairs in back. Most men used the back door to go into Big Gert's, not wanting to be seen going in there. Tom's first stop in town was at the Past Time.

'Hey there, Tom,' Fat Henry called as the cowboy pushed through the swinging doors. 'Hear you got into a little trouble coming down from La Platte. What the hell happened, anyway?'

The best description of the Past Time's owner and bartender, Fat Henry, was the word round. From the top of his pink, shiny, hairless head clear down as far as you wanted to look, he was round. A nose streaked with thin blood veins sat on top of thick, full lips. His chin came in pairs and jiggled like jelly when he laughed, and Fat Henry would laugh at anything and everything. Even the sound he made when talking was big and loud. It was

67

rumored that one time, just after opening the doors to his place of business and breaking open the first cask of bust skull whiskey, a rough and ready cowpoke by the name of Dirty Dan McGrew came in demanding a drink.

Dirty Dan's demeanor didn't please Fat Henry. The saloon owner was hoping to attract the better class of clientele, the ranch owners and their hands. Having a loud, smelly half-drunk pounding at the bar and yelling for a second drink after quickly tossing back the first, caused the owner to frown.

'You haven't paid for the first one yet, sir,' Fat Henry was said to have responded, not moving the bottle he held in his left hand any closer to Dirty Dan's smudged glass.

'Wal, of course not,' Dirty Dan reported snorted indignantly, according to the teller of the story. 'What the hell, ain't the first few drinks of a brand new establishment like this'n on the house?'

For the first and only time in living memory, so the story went, Fat Henry lost his temper. His ever-present smile disappeared and it was his turn to slap a meaty palm flat on the mahogany.

'No, sir,' he is said to have replied, 'this is a business and you will pay for that drink before walking out the door, never to return.'

Dirty Dan guffawed. He was sure he could bluster his way into free drinks. After all it had worked before over at Big Gert's. While the madam wouldn't let him up the stairs, she would pour his glass full before having one or two of her bouncers kick him out the door. He felt sure he could get the same here.

He was wrong. The story gets a little murky at this point in the telling. One or another of the old-timers will start to shake their heads when they hear what happened next, as if they saw things differently but as they like drinking in the Past Time are afraid to argue with the storyteller, Fat Henry himself.

'What happened was Dirty Dan was

a bully. First he cocked a fist like he was going to take a swing at me. Then he changed his mind and drew the longest barreled Colt six-gun I ever did see. Laying it down next to his empty finger-smudged glass, he actually demanded that I pour. Well, gentlemen,' he laughingly beseeched his audience, 'what could I do?' Both chins jiggled as he waited for an answer.

He'd told the story so many times over the years to so many men that most of those hearing it this time knew the answer. Like a chorus, they gave it the same time the bartender did: 'I shot him.' And everyone laughed like it was the biggest joke ever. From that day, if it actually ever happened, to this, Fat Henry was said to laugh at everything, even when pulling the trigger.

Now, standing across the bar from Tom Bantry, he was happily smiling.

Stepping up to the plank bar young Bantry felt the silence in the long narrow room. The handful of men sitting around had heard the greeting and quietly waited to see what developed.

'Now where did you hear about that?' Tom asked nodding when the bartender held up an empty beer mug.

'Sheriff Sullivan came looking for someone to go riding out somewheres yesterday. He mentioned that you had left a dead body laying out there.'

Tom decided not to take it any further. 'Well, then you know everything there is to know. Now then,' he glanced quickly around the room, 'I'm needing half a dozen or so riders to help me build a herd. I figure it'll take pretty much all of three weeks, but we're paying for the full month's work and found.'

'Well, if that doesn't take it all,' a heavy hard voice called from the back of the room. 'But I'd not be so quick to take on this fine offer, boys,' the man said, 'leastways not until I get through with Mr Fast Gun there.'

Tom watched as a big man dressed like a cowhand, denim pants, stovepipe boots, his dirty, sweat-stained Stetson hanging from a thong down his back, moved away from the bar to stand facing him. A gun-heavy belt sagged from his waist putting the cedar handle of a Colt close to the man's right hand.

'Do I know you?' asked Tom softly, straightening up from where he'd been leaning against the bar.

'Nope, we never met, but that don't matter none. My name's Harlan Earle. It was my brother, Rufus that you killed and left there in his bunk. I was the one what found him right where you left him. I buried him and came into town in time to hear the law start talking about someone going out to the shack. I asked and was told what had happened. Hell, I already knew what happened. You killed him. That's what happened.'

Tom tensed. He didn't like the cold, bare way the man was talking.

'I can't deny that,' he said letting his thumb move the thong from his holstered Colt's hammer. 'He seemed to be causing a couple youngsters some trouble. Came at me with a scatter gun with murder in his eye. About all I could do was stop him.'

'Yeah, someone said there was a couple kids out at the cabin. Well, that don't matter none either. You killed Rufus. That's all that matters. Can't let it be known that some fool can get away with that, now can I?'

Earle smiled a little as he asked the question, raising his left hand a little as if searching for the answer. Tom was watching the man's eyes and saw them tighten and was ready when Earle's right hand pulled at his pistol. Tom's gun hand came up filled with the weight of his own six-gun, his thumb letting go of the hammer as the barrel centered on the smiling man's chest. Both guns fired, the two shots sounded like one.

The silence in the long narrow room was total following the crash of gunfire. Both men stood staring at each other, then slowly, as if things had become too heavy for him, Harlan Earle's knees buckled. Fat Henry said later that blood gushed from the man's chest just before he fell face down in the sawdust on the floor.

Instantly the men in the room came alive, telling each other what they had just seen. Tom Bantry felt his knees tremble as he slid his Colt back in the holster and leaned back against the bar.

'Here,' Fat Henry sat a full mug of beer next to Tom's hand. 'Reckon you need this,' he said and then moved away. As the crowd of men moved around, first to take a close look at the dead man and then to move away to order a drink, the bartender found himself nearly swamped. Nobody paid any more attention to Tom.

Hoping no one would notice the quiver of his hand Tom picked the mug up and took a long swallow of the malty brew. He had just put the mug down when the outer door crashed open and Buford Sullivan came rushing in.

'What the hell — ' he started,

stopping to look down at the man lying on his face. 'Well, who's gonna tell me what happened?'

One of the old-timers sitting at a nearby table responded. 'It was as fair a deal as you could want, Sullivan. The big jasper called young Bantry there when he shouldn't of. Said he was gonna make someone pay for killing his brother. Well, he didn't move fast enough, that's what happened.'

Other voices called out, trying to get in on the explanation. Sullivan held up his hand to quiet them down.

'All right, Mose, I see the Colt there in the sawdust. I reckon that's clear enough for me. Now run on over to get the undertaker, will you? If a couple of you men'll carry the body out on to the porch there'll be a beer waiting for you when you get back.'

Helping hands quickly removed the dead man and Sullivan stepped over to stand next to Tom.

'Henry, pour mugs of beer for those fellas, will you? And one for me while I talk to Tom here,' he called to the bartender.

'Well, I should have known,' he said after wiping the foam from his mustache. 'The two of them came into town last night. Told me they'd had to bury their brother and wanted to know who'd shot him. I told them you'd done what you had to do. Had little Bobby and Cora there to back up your story. They didn't say much and I never thought more about it. Guess I should have.'

'Two of them?' Tom asked. 'Where's the other one?'

'Hell, I don't know. I hadn't seen either of them until now.' Looking around the room he shook his head. 'He's not here.'

'Damn-sure hope I don't have another brother hunting me.' Finishing his beer Tom motioned for Fat Henry to fill it up again. 'What'd he look like, big like this one?'

'No, not so you'd notice. I didn't really look at him. This one did all the

76

talking so I didn't pay much attention to the other one. Skinny, as I remember, younger, too. I dunno.'

'Well, I guess it doesn't matter. So, how's your Mattie getting along with Cora and Bobby Lee?'

Sullivan smiled. 'She and that Cora hit it right off. Even with the girl not talking, they seemed to understand each other. Mattie took one look at the dress that young woman was wearing and the heavy coat and took her right in. My fiancée is about the best dressmaker in town, you know. That Cora will be wearing brand new clothes within the hour, I'll bet. Now that Bobby, though, he's something else again. Mattie wanted him to take a bath before going to bed but he wouldn't hear of it. His sister finally took over and grabbing his ear marched him into the kitchen where the tin tub had been filled. I had to laugh when Mattie was telling me about it.'

'What do you think is going to be done with them? I found them and I guess I feel a little responsible.'

'I don't know. Mattie told me not to worry about it. She said that things would work out. I don't see what she's thinking about, but I've learned to trust her. Oh, and I got to warn you, that Cora Lee ain't no little girl, either. She's only a year or so younger than Mattie. And,' he said more excitedly, 'guess what, their last name ain't Lee. That's both their middle names. Bobby Lee Carlyle and Cora Lee Carlyle. Bobby told Mattie that. Wouldn't say where their parents are or if they've got any relatives around the country, but he did tell us their last names. I've sent telegrams over to La Platte to see what they can tell us.'

'That Cora Lee still isn't talking, I take it.'

'Not a word. Mattie said she was giving up trying to get something out of her. Said every time she thought the girl was about to speak her face would get all hard and kinda dark, you know? And that was all.'

The two men stood for a time, not talking, both thinking their own thoughts.

'Well, as much as I'd like to visit, guess I'd better get on with finding some hands.'

'That shouldn't be too hard. There're five or six men came into town this morning. They'd been working out at the Davis spread. Too bad about that. Remember I mentioned them the other day? Horace and Lucinda Davis? A fine couple and that Horace seemed to be on top of things, raising a good little herd of blooded stock. But I guess when a man's luck isn't running in his favor it just wasn't meant to be.'

'Yeah, I remember you talking about them. Raising horses somewhere over east of here, wasn't he? What happened?'

'That's right. It was when Sidwell asked me to deliver some papers out to the Davis place. Well, it seems Horace had borrowed money using a dozen or so head of young stallions for security. That note came due and the papers Sidwell had were official foreclosure notices. Damn, I hated to do it. I really liked them people. But Sidwell had done it right, got his lawyer to draw up the papers and telegraphed them to the judge up at the county seat for him to sign. All I could do was deliver them. Sure makes me wonder if I like wearing this badge.'

'Now that's not thinking, Buford, you're perfect for the job, at least for the people in Ferris Corners. But why didn't Davis simply sell enough stock to cover the loan?'

'He couldn't. We've had a bunch of rustling going on around here lately. Nobody losing much, and then mostly from those spreads farther down to the south. A few head here and a small herd there. I wired the sheriff a couple weeks or maybe a month ago and he said he'd send someone down to look into it. Nobody's come around, though and, well, hell, I can't do anything. All I'm good for is keeping things quiet here in town. Anyway, just a few nights ago the rustlers hit the Davis spread. Ran off close to two dozen head. All the year-lings that'd been up in one pasture and most of the stud horses he had in another. It was the yearlings he was counting on to sell to clear the bank loan.'

'It was a loan through Silas?'

'Yep.'

'Foreclosing on a loan like that doesn't sound like something he'd do, not Silas Sidwell.'

'All I can say is, it isn't something his pa would have done, foreclosing on them like that. The old man wanted this country to grow and he was always willing to let some things slide a little if he had to, to keep the right people here. The Davises were the right people, too. But young Silas, well, he sees things differently, I guess.'

Tom nodded slowly. 'Yeah,' he said, almost to himself, 'I guess he does.'

* * *

Before all the shooting had started, nobody had been paying any attention

81

to the man who'd been sitting alone at a table over against the far wall. When it was all over he'd been one of the first to go to take a good look at the dead man. Not saying anything, just shaking his head, the man turned back to his table.

'Damn,' Victor Garrett muttered as he picked up his half-empty beer mug and finished it off.

Garrett had been on the trail for nearly two months and this was the closest he'd gotten to any of Stokey's men since the gun battle back on the trail out of Ophir. The man lying in the sawdust of the Past Time floor was one of the Earle brothers. Garrett thought at least one of the brothers had been riding with Stokey at the time of the last gold hold-up.

The manhunter was in Ferris Corners because that was where Harlan and Rufus Earle were said to be hanging out. The Earle brothers — he had thought there had only been two of them but someone up in La Platte said there were three — were thought to be busy in the Ferris

Corners basin. At one time, over in Ophir, one of the Earle boys had been seen to be riding with Stokey. That outlaw's name hadn't come up but Garrett had decided to ride south just to check it out. Listening around town he'd heard all about the rustling that was going on. Well, maybe it wasn't too late yet to cash in on that reward for Hard Luck Hank Stokey.

8

Finding six men looking for work turned out to be easy; by the time Tom Bantry and the deputy sheriff finished their second glass of beer, four men came up to the bar.

Buford Sullivan, put his empty beer mug on the mahogany and shook his head at Fat Henry.

'No more for me, right now at least. I still got the shooting to write up. Sheriff Curtis over in La Platte has a new rule that everything has to be reported. I don't know what he's thinking, but I expect a shooting is one of those things. Tom, stop by Mattie's and see the Carlyles if you want. But watch yourself. As I said, that Cora Lee ain't no little girl.'

Chuckling to himself the lawman pushed out through the swinging doors.

The four men had been sitting at a

table near the back wall and had seen the shooting. Tom thought at first that was what they wanted to talk about. He was surprised when it was the job. Surprised and pleased.

'Boys, that takes a load off my mind. Even if we don't find a couple more men, with you four we'll be able to make up that herd in time to get them to the cattle cars I ordered.' They had no more than introduced themselves when another rider came in wanting to talk about a job.

'You Tom Bantry?' he asked stopping in front of Tom. 'I just saw the deputy sheriff out there and he said you might be hiring.'

The fifth man said his name was Billy Horton and that he, along with the other four, had until yesterday worked out at the Davis ranch.

'It was a cruel blow,' Horton said, 'them losing the place like that. Horace and Lucinda Davis are right nice people. Good to work for and always paid their hands on time. It's a crying shame to lose all that hard work they'd put into the ranch.'

The other men murmured in agreement.

Tom told his new crew to get their gear together and head out to the Flying B. He'd be along a little later, he said, but there were a couple things in town he had to see to.

'Just tell Pa or Lafe when you get there that I hired you and that we'll start out early in the morning.'

Watching the men ride out, Tom was turning toward the bank on the other side of the street when a thin young man called to him from the far corner of the bank building.

'Hey, there mister, wait up a minute,' he said, almost Tom thought, making it an order. 'I hear you're looking for a few men for a while. I could use the work.'

Tom smiled. This would give them the full crew he needed to get his herd gathered. Looking the newcomer over though, he paused. Up close he saw how ragged his clothes were and how young he was. From the patches on the knees of the youngster's pants, Tom wondered if he'd been working too long in a garden somewhere.

'Well,' he hesitated, 'yes, I've just hired a crew to help out for a few weeks. Guess I'm not sure if I need any more men.'

'I could sure use the work, mister. Been working out at, uh, my pa's place and he up and died on me. I got no place to go and nothing to do when I get there. I can ride and, guess I don't look it, but I know my way around horses. I could take care of your remuda for you. You got enough hands to make a gather they'll need a slew of mounts, won't they? Well, I'm your man for that job.'

Tom had to laugh at his persistence. 'All right, you're hired. It'll only be for about three weeks, but get your gear together and follow those men out. I'll be along later.'

'Thanks a lot, mister. You won't

regret it.' The youngster turned away before mentioning his name. Tom had wanted to ask how old he was too, but decided that would have to wait too.

Entering the bank, Tom nodded to the young clerk standing behind the high counter. 'Morning, is Silas in?'

'Back through that door.'

Tom buried his smile. The first time he'd come into the bank with his pa he'd been, oh, six or maybe seven years old. Through the time he and Silas were growing up and going to school, they'd played cowboys and robbers in the bank many rainy afternoons. He well knew where the banker's office was.

Pushing through the heavy wooden door without knocking, he was stopped by an angry growl. 'Damn it, I told you not to bother me right now,' Silas Sidwell said, his deep frown disappearing into a smile when he saw who it was.

'Ah, hell, Tom. Come on in. Sorry about yelling like that but it seems those two knuckleheads out there can't think for themselves, always busting in here with some idiot question or another. Pull up a chair and let's talk. You know, we just don't spend enough time together any more. Guess with you running the Flying B and me trying to keep things going along here, there just aren't enough days in the week.'

'Well, I guess,' Tom sighed. 'I don't know much about banking but I'm here to tell you, ranching is a full-time job. But that's what I wanted to talk to you about, banking. I've been hearing how things have changed here in the bank. It isn't any of my business, but your foreclosing on the Davis horse ranch hits close to home. Like them I've got a loan with you that a small herd will be going to market to pay off. I don't ever recall your pa foreclosing on a loan like that.'

'No, he never did and that's the problem I'm having now. Tom, you're right, there's a lot to making a bank profitable that people don't know about. Take that loan Horace Davis took out. It was too big for the size of his operation. I tried to tell him that when he came in but he said he needed that much money in order to expand his breeding stock. Well, I did what I could, but the bank has to show a profit. It hurts me to have to send Deputy Sheriff Sullivan out there, but' — holding his hands out, palms up, pleadingly — 'that's what can happen in business when things aren't managed right.'

'Buford said the Davis loan was based on the sale of a herd of stock but the horses got stolen. That's the same plan I have, to pay off the loan by sending a small herd to market end of the month.'

Sidwell chuckled. 'Well, Tom, I don't think there's anything you should worry about, do you? I mean your loan wasn't so big that you can't clear it up with a hundred head or so. Anyway, if trouble did hit, we could always rewrite the note.'

Tom wasn't sure he felt better about

it. He and his father had talked about the need to borrow but Asa Bantry had never worked on borrowed money and didn't like being in debt. His son, however, saw it differently. Using the bank's money for a couple months in order to purchase that piece of land back up in the high country would nearly double the ranch's water supply. When old man Harvey had ridden down to tell Asa that he was selling out, he was giving the Bantrys the first opportunity to buy. Tom argued that it was an opportunity not to pass up. The trip up to the county seat had been to register the sale. So far nobody except the principals in the deal knew of it. Tom wanted to keep it that way for a while.

'Well,' he nodded, 'you're right. I guess there's not anything for me to worry about. I've been able to hire half a dozen men and we won't have any trouble making our gather.'

Coming to his feet, he reached across the desk to shake Silas's hand. 'Just wanted to hear what you had to say about it, Silas. And you're right. I get this deal completed and we'll have to spend a few days up at one of the high lakes, catching trout.'

The banker smiled. 'Well, that'd be real nice. Don't know when I'll be able to take the time away from the bank, though. Training those two out there is taking longer than I thought it would.'

Tom wondered why he hadn't kept at least one of the older men who'd worked at the bank since God was a pup to help train the new ones, but didn't ask. It wasn't, he decided, any of his business. Silas told him anyhow.

'I thought about keeping Uriah on for a while but those two old fellers were thinking they knew best how I should be running the bank. They couldn't see that my father's way just wasn't as profitable as the changes I wanted to make. I hated to do it, but I had to let them both go. And now I have to spend time trying to keep everything running smoothly. Ah, well, it'll all be worth it, I'm certain.'

Tom nodded and, waving a hand, walked out.

One more stop, he thought, heading around toward the back street, and he'd head for the home place. Likely be there in time for supper. He'd keep the visit with Mattie Andrews and her two house guests short, he told himself.

* * *

Cora Lee answered the door when he knocked. Seeing who it was, she stepped aside and, keeping her head down, waited for Tom to enter the little house before closing the door.

'Who is it, Cora?' he heard Mattie call, followed by an exclamation. 'Oh, blast! I do wish that girl would talk.' Coming into the living room, Mattie was holding her flour-coated hands up. Seeing Tom she smiled.

'Oh, it's you. And how did you know I was baking? Well, don't just stand there, come on back to the kitchen and see what Cora and I have been doing.'

The big wooden table took up most of the kitchen floor; the table top was covered with flour. A large lump of dough was lying on the coated flat surface.

'How long to knead the dough, is the question I used to ask my ma back when I was a girl and she was making bread. Just long enough, she'd say. I never did find out and now I'm making bread and still don't know the answer. Well, sit down and have a cup of coffee and watch us work. Cora, will you get Tom Bantry a cup, please?'

Tom had to marvel in the change he saw in the girl. Watching her move to the stove and pour a mug of coffee he realized he'd have to change the way he thought about her. Somehow Cora no longer looked like a youngster but more like a grown woman. Maybe it was the dress. The last time he saw her she was wearing a faded shapeless cotton shift of a dress. That was a long way from what he saw on her now.

'That dress you're admiring,' Mattie laughed, 'is one of mine. She fits into it right nice, wouldn't you say?'

'Uh-huh,' was all Tom felt safe in answering. 'Yes, Miss Cora Lee has gone through a change, that's for sure.' Even while she was being talked about, the young woman didn't show any sign of paying attention.

'I see she still won't talk. I wonder what that's all about.'

Mattie, giving the mound of dough a final slap, shook her head. 'I can't figure it out. We had Doc Lewis over yesterday and he checked both Cora and Bobby over. He couldn't find anything wrong with either of them, but he didn't have an answer.'

'Speaking of Bobby, where is that little scoundrel?'

'You described him right,' she laughed. 'He's a real scallywag. He's supposed to be out chopping firewood. Making bread is an all day affair and it takes a lot of wood for the stove. He didn't like the idea but when I told him I was also making an apple pie, he decided it'd be all right to help out.'

Sipping the hot coffee, Tom watched the two women work, one talking almost continuously and the other silent. Having the pressure of hiring a crew off his shoulders, and sitting in a warm, sweet-smelling kitchen with two young women to watch at work, helped him relax.

Thinking about the work that had to be done out at the ranch, he shook himself and, finishing his coffee, stood up.

'I hate to leave when I know there's an apple pie coming, but there's still too much back at the ranch to get done for me to be lollygagging around. I just wanted to stop in and see how Cora and Bobby were. I don't suppose anyone has come forward to claim them, have they?'

'No, and I somehow don't think there will be. Bobby won't say much, but from what little bit I or Buford have been able to get out of him, it seems likely I'll have house guests for a while. And welcome they are, too. I really enjoy having Cora here, she's a big help even if we can't gossip. Bobby helps out a lot too, although he talks enough for both of them. Doesn't say anything worth while, mind you, just chatters away like a little monkey.'

Tom had to laugh, catching Cora glance up at him before quickly looking back at the bread dough she had started kneading.

'That's good.' Putting his hat squarely on his head he nodded, 'I'll stop back by in a few days to see how things are going. Tell Buford I'll talk to him then.'

Stepping out onto the narrow porch, Tom halted and took a long look around. Nothing, as far as he could tell, was out of place but he had the feeling that something wasn't right.

'Ah hell, you're just being goosey,' he said to himself and then frowned, remembering something Buford had said. The man he'd shot in the saloon had a younger brother, the deputy sheriff said, but nobody knew where he was. Maybe, Tom decided, he'd better be a little more cautious.

9

Silas Sidwell watched Tom Bantry come out of the livery stable and lead his horse over to a water trough that sat between the hotel and the general store.

'There he is now,' the slender man standing in his scuffed and shabby boots next to the banker muttered. 'I could cut out back and get him when he rides out. He'd never know what hit him.'

Sidwell scowled. 'How many times do I have to say it? Leave Bantry alone!' he ordered gruffly. Noticing the look in the man's eye, he softened his tone. 'At least for now. You'll get your chance but the time isn't right, yet.'

'You keep saying that, do this and do that. It just don't make no sense. Rufus and Harlan didn't understand it and now they're dead. And there goes the jasper what shot both of them. It ain't clear to me why I gotta wait.'

'Look, I told you how hard it's going to be, now with your brothers dead. But that just puts more in your pocket. Yeah,' he held up a hand to stop the other man from cutting in, 'I know. It'll make it harder for you, a lot more work. It'll be worth it though, trust me. And part of it is letting Bantry do what he's doing. You'll get your chance at him, but not until the time is right. Now, get outa here and do what I told you. And damnit, ride carefully. The wrong people see you and they'll get ideas. Do it like I said and we're home free. You'll get your revenge and I'll get what I want and we'll both be happy.'

Scowling, the lean man nodded and headed for the door. 'All right. Harlan was sure this was a good plan so I'll go along. But it'd better work out like you say or I'll be coming back to talk to you again.'

Sidwell could only nod as the back door to his office slammed closed.

When everything was done, he said

to himself, and he had what he wanted, something would have to be done about that young fool.

* * *

Until he'd been told differently by that feller up at the county seat who seemed to know, Victor Garrett had always thought there were only two Earle brothers. Even back in Ophir he'd heard something about one of them taking up with the Stokey gang. Well, Garrett knew what that wild bunch had been doing, didn't he? Since he was hired by the miners' committee to put a stop to the bastards that'd been robbing the gold shipments he'd found out something about that gang.

Hank Stokey had been pretty well known down around the southern part of the state as a minor outlaw. According to what everyone had ever heard most of the real bad men riding the back trails laughed at his efforts. Stokey just wasn't smart enough to pull off anything worthwhile. Somewhere he'd picked up the nickname and was known as Hard Luck Stokey.

The reason, again according to bar room gossip, was that the handle had come from the time he stood in the middle of the wagon road, a faded blue bandanna pulled up over his nose and a Colt .45 in each hand. When the stage carrying the mail with Micah Welch handling the ribbons came around the bend the would-be hold-up man had fired one pistol into the air, yelling for the stage to stop. Old Micah didn't even hesitate. He'd been driving stage coaches for going on ten years, through all kinds of weather and over all kinds of roads. There had been only once that any stage he was piloting was held up. And that time it took a big log across the road and five or six men, he never was sure, all pointing firearms at him, to do it.

Well, that time the bandits got away with a couple hundred dollars and most of that had come from a puffed-up dude passenger who just wouldn't stop yammering. The way Micah told the story, the dude made a big deal of how important he was, showing off a little card that proved he was part-owner in the stage line and got to ride free.

'Of course,' Micah sighed in the telling, 'when he reached for the leather billfold to get the card, he had to dig behind a wad of money, good old greenbacks, to get to it. Up to that point the blamed hold-up men were only interested in the strong box. Damn fool dude all but handed them his money. Weren't nothing worthwhile in the strong box on that trip, neither.'

Well, when Micah saw the lone, masked hold-up man standing square in the middle of the road firing his handguns at the clouds he did the only thing he could do: he snapped the whip over the heads of the lead team and barreled right over the masked man. When he told the sheriff in the next town about it, describing the outlaw as being thin and stoop-shouldered and carrying two Colts, the sheriff knew right off who it was. That description fit only one man, Hank Stokey. He'd had Stokey in one of the cells recently, charged with trying to rob the Chinese laundryman.

'A joke, that's what he is,' the lawman snorted. 'He was being chased down the street by a very angry Chinese man who was waving a three-foot long sword when I caught him. I had to put Hank in jail just to save his sorry neck from that mad foreigner.'

The story of the failed stage hold-up made the rounds and had everyone smirking whenever Stokey came by. It was soon after that when folks started calling him Hard Luck Hank. It didn't take long for him to take his penny ante crimes north, ending up in Ophir.

There had been quite a bit of gold taken from the hills around that little gold strike. It wasn't ever going to be as big as Sutter's Mill out in California, or the diggings down in the Comstock Lode country. All big mineral finds anywhere had things in common, though. Naturally, when someone found gold in the ground the next day there'd be a whole raft of people coming by, ready to get as much of it as they could. These were the kind of people, mostly men but not always, who knew it was often easier to take it from those who had dug it out of the ground than it was to do the digging themselves.

For once luck was with Hard Luck Hank Stokey. He got a few men to back him and his newly formed gang was successful in holding up a wagon carrying a load of rough smelted gold bars headed for La Platte and the nearest bank.

The second time that he and four other hard cases stopped a wagon carrying a big chest, secure with locks and steel straps, they weren't so fortunate. To make matters worse, one of the two guards riding alongside thought he recognized the leader who was giving the orders.

'Yeah, I'll swear it was that fool,

Stokey,' the guard testified later to a small crowd lining the bar in the Ophir Saloon. 'And I heard somewheres that Half-breed Charlie is running with him now.'

A second man standing there listening called out his information. 'Well, if 'n that's Charlie then you can figure Curry's with him. They been partnering for some time.'

The guard didn't like losing his audience. Quickly he tried to get the attention back his way. 'You want to know something else, boys? Something funny?' he asked, raising his voice above the others. 'The jokes on those blamed fool hold-up men. That box taking up the rear of the wagon what we was protecting was empty. Yes sir, it was one of them — what do you call it? — a hoax. Weren't nothing worth anything in there. We was the decoy shipment. While we made a big thing of riding toward the county seat, someone with a couple packhorses was going over the high passes. Ha, I tell you, you shoulda seen their faces when they got them locks broken open.'

'Wal, if that don't take the cake,' another man said, laughing long and loud. 'That tears it. For sure it was Hard Luck Hank Stokey.'

Harlan and Rufus Earle had been sitting in at one of the poker tables toward the back when this tale was told. The elder brother had thrown in his hand and while waiting for the next hand overheard the talk. He'd been trying to hook up with Stokey ever since hearing about the gold shipment the outlaw gang had taken a few weeks earlier. Neither of the Earle boys was a good poker player and making any kind of living with cards wasn't doing the trick.

The brothers had talked about getting some of the gold that was floating around but hadn't come up with a way to do it until they heard about Stokey. Harlan had talked to Rufus, trying to get him to go back to the cabin. Riding the outlaw trail wasn't something his younger brother could do easily, he thought. Anyway, it was part of his duty to protect Rufus, wasn't it? The brothers had found the sorry run-down cabin over on the other side of the Ferris Corners basin a year or so before. It was a real hardscrabble place; the ramshackle cabin was close to falling down. A nearby pasture provided grass for their horses but it wasn't big enough to put any stock on. The place wouldn't put any food on the table but it was better than sleeping outside all the time.

'There you go, gentlemen.' One of the other players, a miner from the looks of his clothes, slapped down his cards and, showing a pair of aces, pulled the pot his way. 'That's the best hand I've had all day.'

The player, obviously a miner, had said his name was Edgar something, but Harlan hadn't been paying any attention. All the big man was doing was filling his time until he could figure out a way to meet up with Stokey. From what he'd heard here today he may be close to getting what he wanted. He'd ridden once with a no-good feller who called himself Kid Curry and he'd know him anywhere. Leaning close to Rufus's head, Harlan said he was leaving.

'I got things to do, Rufus. C'mon, I'm outa here and don't you be hanging around long either. You take yourself back to the cabin and I'll be by in a couple days. I'll see if I can't bring a sack of grub. Go on over to the cabin and don't let anyone see you, you hear?'

Rufus didn't move, but nodded. 'I'll be along in a minute or two,' and watched his brother walk out of the saloon.

Rufus had been listening when the miner had said his name. Someone had mentioned that this Edgar feller was one of the owners of a claim somewhere up the canyon.

'Look you gonna play, or what?' Edgar snarled, waiting for Rufus to ante up before dealing the next hand.

'Naw, I've had enough.' He wanted to get this jasper outside.

Edgar wasn't having it. 'You been taking my money all afternoon and now you just want to walk away before I got a chance to get some of it back?'

Edgar was drunk. He'd started drinking the cheap rotgut sold by the bottle from behind the bar since noon. But he'd also won the last hand or two and was feeling like his luck had turned. The other players, knowing it was the liquor talking, settled back to see what Earle would do. It was easy to tell that the drunk miner was out of his league; Rufus Earle was not only cold sober, he was known to be short-tempered.

'Mister,' Earle sat back and stared hard at the drunk. 'I don't care a bit about how much you've won or, for that matter, lost. It ain't enough to worry me. Now if you really want to push your luck, keep smart-talking and I'll sober you up in a hurry.'

'Oh, yeah, you're a big bad one, ain't

you. All right, I'll tell you what, let's me and you cut the cards, high card wins.'

Earle chuckled. 'And what you putting in the pot, that little pile you got in front of you?'

Edgar sat looking at his money. It wasn't much. Until recently he'd had pocketfuls to carry around. But his luck had faded. What was in front of him was all he had and he still had to pay his hotel bill and feed his family. Family, he almost started to cry at that thought. His wife had died leaving him with his girl and the youngster. It wasn't a good place to be, having a girl near old enough to marry and a boy just coming on, and no mother to teach them right. And a pa whose luck had changed.

'Well, what the hell you gonna do?' Earle snarled, placing his hands on the arms of the chair, started to rise. 'Set there and brood or make it worth my while?'

Edgar nodded. He had to come out of this with enough to pay the bills and get out of town. 'All I got is right there. But there's a couple horses down at the livery, both good animals. And there's my wagon, too, a ranch wagon. I'll put up everything I got against the cash money you took off this table today.'

Earle smirked. 'A couple horses more to feed ain't what I need. But to get you off my back, I'll put, let's see — ' Slowly he pushed a handful of coins into the center of the table. Looking up he saw the greed in Edgar's eyes when he picked up a stack of greenbacks. Slowly counting out the bills, he nearly laughed at the look on the other man's face. 'OK, that's it. There's a hundred dollars in the pile. That's against what you got there and, as you say, everything you got.' Glancing at one of the other players, he nodded. 'You,' he pointed a finger at one of the other men, 'shuffle the cards.'

Quickly the cards were shuffled and squared up. 'OK,' said Earle smiling coldly, 'it's your call. You do your best, high card takes the pot.'

Slowly as if realizing he'd bet it all, Edgar picked up a little more than half the deck, turning over to show a jack of spades. A good high face card. He smiled at his good luck.

Not wasting any time, Earle took nearly all of what was left, turning the short stack over face up on the table. The ace of hearts.

'Now,' the winner said, putting the bills back in his pocket and picking up the coins, 'let's go look at those horses I just won.'

10

Garrett recognized Harlan Earle when the outlaw had ridden bold as brass tacks into Ferris Corners. He remembered seeing him with that other Earle, Rufus, over in Ophir, especially when Rufus had won at poker. That alone hadn't been enough to make him remember, but when the loser in that game had killed himself, it had. Somehow Garrett thought everything about that sorry deal hadn't been made clear.

He recalled how, when Rufus Earle had ridden out of town, he was sitting high on the seat of his newly acquired wagon. That was the last time Garrett remembered seeing the big brute of a man but the two looked a lot alike so he had no trouble making out Harlan. Anyway, he'd been told by that old man down at the livery that Harlan Earle had joined up with Stokey.

Garrett almost shouted with happiness, when Harlan and some young skinny rider had ridden into town. He couldn't recall ever seeing the young feller riding alongside the big man and didn't really pay any attention to him. Harlan Earle, he thought, could be his ticket to finding Stokey and that man was the one he focused on.

Garrett's first thought when Harlan found himself face down in the sawdust was that it was the end of the trail for finding Stokey. But then he remembered the skinny kid. That could possibly be the third Earle brother. Not exactly sure what he looked like, Garrett sat out on the hotel porch the rest of the day, eyeballing every young skinny rider that went by. Finally spotting what looked like his man, Garrett watched him going around the corner of the bank. Stepping quickly over to that corner, he watched the youngster disappear into the back door of the building. There was something sneaky about the way the kid was moving. Garrett decided to wait around.

Waiting was easy for Garrett. He was hunting the reward and that kid just might lead him to it.

★　★　★

The next two weeks went by fast for Tom Bantry and Lafe Gunnison. While Asa fretted at being left behind, his son and the hands slowly got together the herd they wanted. The price Tom had been quoted when he last talked with a buyer meant that it'd take slightly more than a hundred head to raise enough cash money for the loan. Wanting to take only the older stock, leaving yearlings and two-year-olds for the spring round-up, called for careful culling. All the hands, with the exception of the youngster in charge of the remuda, knew enough about cattle to know what to look for. The herd was building quicker than either Tom or Lafe had thought possible.

'Guess that means there's too much old stuff on the range,' Lafe pointed out at supper that night. He had taken over as camp cook, having set up the chuck wagon in the little valley the make-up herd was being held in. The two men sat with their backs to a fallen log, across the campfire from the rest of the hands.

Tom nodded. 'That means we'll have to do a better job during the next round-up. But that's something to think about then, not now. You know,' he went on after a while, 'I think we're doing so well it wouldn't hurt for me to take a little look-see over to the east range. The beeves we been getting are mostly from this side and it'd likely be a good idea to have an idea of what's over there.'

'Humph, someone's wanting to get out of the fun of chasing contrary animals, I'd say.'

The younger man laughed. 'Yep, sounds like it to me, too. But you have to admit, it's been, what, six months

116

since any of us has been over there? Well, three or four anyway. I'll just mosey along. Someone'll have to see what the conditions are before winter anyhow. I'm thinking, once we get this herd to the railhead and pay off the bank, there'll be enough money to keep on a man or two over winter. Put them out along the property line, pushing back whatever they find.'

Lafe didn't say anything while he used a piece of bread to wipe up the drippings from the tin plate. 'Yeah. You know with all that talk about rustling going on, it might turn out there ain't no stock out there to turn back.'

'Buford told me that is more likely to be the case down to the south. He didn't mention any stock being lost up this way.'

'How would we know? Haven't seen anything much from those ranches over along the east wall, have you?'

'No, guess not. Well, I'll take an extra horse and take a *paseo* in that direction come morning.'

'Whoa up there. How about you ride into town first? I figure we'll be out here another week at least. That means I'll need coffee and flour, hell, I'll make you up a list. You can put off taking your afternoon stroll without a worry if 'n I got enough grub to feed these rannies.'

'Hey,' one of the men sitting on the other side of the fire called out, 'if you're heading for town, could you bring me a sack of tobacco? I'm nearly out.' Tom saw it was Billy Horton asking.

'You're too young to be smoking, Billy,' another hand called. 'Mr Lafe, sir,' the man went on, 'how about you putting a couple bottles of whiskey on your list. In case of snake bite, you understand.'

Laughing, one after another the men started joshing each other.

★　★　★

Tom was just about finished with his morning coffee early the next day when

Horton wandered away from the chuckwagon to settle down on his heels next to the rancher.

'It likely ain't any of my business, boss, but did you know that scruffy-looking horse wrangler you hired was gone most of the night? I don't want to tell tales outa school but I did notice him gone from his soogans when I took over my turn at nighthawking. I figured he'd gone out to the remuda but when I rode around the rope corral he'd set up to hold the horses there was no sign of him. But he's over there this morning, looking half asleep. Don't know if it means anything, just thought you'd like to know.'

Watching the man walk back to dump his cup in the wash tub, Tom thought about the horse wrangler. Why, he asked himself, would anyone want to be night riding? Sneaking into town for a drink or to see a woman was the most likely answer but the round-up camp was a good day's ride away. Shaking his head, he let it go. As long as the whip-sawed looking feller did his job, what he did other times was his own business.

Sitting on the back of a black stud horse, with Lafe's shopping list in a shirt pocket, Tom rode out of camp, heading for Ferris Corners.

It was a beautiful morning, cool with just the first hint of fall in the air. Somewhere along the way a covey of quail rose up in flight from under the stud's hoofs, making the horse scamper sideways and bringing a smile to Tom's face. It was, he decided, a good day to be alive.

Coming into town in time for supper, he headed straight for the Mexican's restaurant. Smiling at a few of the seated customers Tom saw Buford sitting at a table near the back and went to join him.

'Hey, looky here,' the deputy sheriff howled, 'if it isn't the north country's favorite rancher. Come in for some good cooking? That must mean old Lafe's falling down on the job.'

Tom had to laugh. 'Nope, came in to see my favorite overworked lawman. And I knew you'd be either here or over at the Past Time.'

'Where I'll be soon as I finish up here. And,' he dragged out the word, 'you'll be just in time to buy the first drink.'

Sullivan cleaned up his meal and waited while Tom had ordered his before speaking. 'What's new out at the Flying B. You getting that herd you was talking about all gathered?'

'Yeah, it's going along pretty good. We should be ready to start driving them this way in a few more days. Boy, I'll be glad when it's over. We've been working our butts off, I'll tell you. What's new in town that I should know about?'

The smile left Sullivan's face. 'There's been more reports of rustlers hitting the outlying ranches. Nobody seems to see anything and what I'm told, there's no sign of who's doing it or how many there are or anything. I sent another wire to the sheriff but he doesn't appear to have anyone to send down. The next thing I can think of doing is to send over to the state capital, to the marshal's office.' Shaking his head, 'I just don't know what else to do.'

'I'm thinking about taking a little ride over our east range when I get back out to the ranch. It dawned on me that there might not be anything out there; your rustlers might have already cleaned it out. We don't use that range much, it's not as wet country as the main range or what's up in the foothills. Next spring we'll be covering that area first.'

'That doesn't seem to be the way they work. From all reports they wait until a jag of stock is all gathered up and then take 'em. Leastways that's what it looks like they do.'

'Well, if someone's got a herd all made up, it'd be easier to run them off than going out to make your own round-up, I guess.'

'Don't be overlooking the fact that you're putting together a nice little gather.'

'Oh, I'm not. We've got a pretty good holding ground we're using. It's a tight little valley with good water and grass. It's basically only got one way in and one out. I think we're protected. Anyway, that crew isn't someone to mess with. They're pretty savvy men. In any case, we're about done. The way things are going I'd say we'll be making our drive to the rail yard in another week at the latest.'

'And then you can sit back and take life easy. Well, that's good. And there you have it. That's all the news.' Sullivan hesitated a bit before going on, 'There is one other thing. It's about something your banker friend is doing. You know old Angus Ridgeway, down at the telegraph office? He tells me Sidwell has been sending more telegrams to the judge's office over in La Platte. Old Angus isn't suppose to tell people what's in other folks' wires but he gets a little lonely and he does like to talk. Well, he said it bothered him some when he saw the names on the banker's telegrams. He wouldn't tell me who all the names were on them, though. Said he didn't want anyone knowing he'd told me. Said I'd know as soon as young Sidwell came to have me serve the official papers. Damn thing is, if he gets the judge to sign off on any more foreclosures I gotta deliver 'em. That's part of my job.'

'Yeah, Silas does have a different idea of what a small town banker is supposed to do. I purely hate to see what he's doing, though.'

'C'mon, Tom, all this talk is making me thirsty. I'll bust for the first beer.'

11

Tom took a room at the hotel and stayed in town that night. Before leaving for the ranch the next morning he rode by Mattie Andrews's place to check up on Bobby and his sister.

'Hey, Mister Tom,' Bobby called as the cowboy tied the reins to the front fence and pushed through the gate. 'I been hoping you'd come along. I need your help with something.'

'Morning, Bobby. What can I help you with?'

'It's that woman you and the deputy sheriff stuck us with. I can't talk to him 'cause he's gonna marry Miss Mattie and he don't want to do nothing against what she wants. You're the only other one who'll listen. Will you help me?'

'Well, I don't know. What seems to be the problem?'

'She wants me to start going to the school they got here. I tried to tell her I don't need no citified dude trying to tell me things, things I don't need like writing or reading some funny stories a dead man wrote. Worse thing is, Cora had to go and agree with her. Blast it, I don't know what else to do but get you to help me talk them out this foolishness. Will you? Both o' them are back there in the kitchen working up to do some cooking. That's another thing, they's always cooking something or another and I'm the one what's got to pack in the firewood. Darn and tarnation, it's just too much.'

Tom fought to keep a straight face. 'Well, Bobby I'll tell you straight, when it comes to women you just got to give in and let them drive the coach. First off, a little schooling won't hurt any youngster. I'd say the best thing is to let your sister and Miss Mattie have their way. Sooner or later they're apt to forget all about it and meddle in other things. Far as fetching firewood, well, didn't I hear something about an apple pie the last time I was in town?'

'Yeah, that was a couple days ago. Really good pie, you missed out.'

'Uh-huh. Course I didn't pack any firewood so unless Miss Mattie or your sister invited me I wouldn't likely get any of the pie. You did though 'cause you helped out. Now don't you think it's right that you help them with their work seeing as how you're getting to eat the food they cook?'

'Well, maybe. But, golly, I'd rather go fishing. Will you take me fishing?'

'Yep, we can do that. As soon as I get a herd sold we'll go. Meanwhile I think I'll have a little talk with the women before I head back to the ranch. You say they're inside?'

'Yeah,' the boy said disgustedly. 'OK, if you say I should get bringing in firewood I will. I don't want to, but I will.'

★ ★ ★

Cora Lee was wearing a different dress, one that Tom had to be careful not to stare at. It was clear this was not a young girl.

'Tom, it's good of you to stop by,' Mattie Andrews said happily as he came into the kitchen. 'We've got fresh coffee on but I'm afraid you're too late for any of that apple pie we made the other day. That Bobby just couldn't keep his hands off it till it was all gone.'

Tom chuckled. 'Yeah, we just had a little talk. Seems he doesn't think too much of the idea of going to school.' Trying to keep his eyes off the way Cora's dress fit her, he almost missed seeing her glance at him out of the corner of her eye. The look was fleeting before she turned her gaze on the bowl she was stirring.

'If you stick around a while,' Mattie said, smiling at what she saw, 'there'll be a chocolate cake coming out of the oven. Cora is a real good cook.'

'Now that sounds perfect, but I've got a herd to see to. Maybe after all this work gets done I'll get another invite.'

Cora didn't look up, but continued to stir the batter.

'Doesn't she look nice in that dress?' Mattie asked. 'It's another one I hadn't worn in a long time. Cora had to do a little sewing to make it fit, but it sure looks good on her, doesn't it?'

Tom just nodded.

'It's funny,' Mattie went on, 'she can cook, sew and likes to clean up. But for all that, she won't say a word. She and Bobby get along all right without her talking, but it certainly doesn't make things easy for me, I'll tell you. There are so many things I'd like to hear her tell me. Cora,' she turned to the young woman, 'won't you even try to say something to Tom?'

Cora kept her head down and continued to stir the cake batter.

'That's all right,' Tom said after a moment. 'I reckon she'll talk when she wants to. Anyhow, I'm glad you're all getting along so well together. And that Bobby is going to go to school.

Somehow I feel a little responsible for them and it's a relief to know they're being taken care of. Well, I'll be on my way. Good day to you, Miss Cora Lee.'

'I'll walk you out, Tom,' Mattie said, taking his arm.

Stopping on the front porch the woman looked up at the cowboy. 'I tease her shamelessly,' Mattie said softening her tone. 'It probably doesn't sound good but I'm just trying to get her to talk. I don't think it troubles her much.'

Tom adjusted his wide-brimmed hat and chuckled.

'I'll say this, she can cook, bake and sew. I have to admit she's very pretty in that dress. It'd be too much if it turned out that she could not only speak but could sing too. You'd have a hard time keeping all the young men in the basin away from her.'

'And I'll bet you'd be at the front of the pack. Now, get on with you. I've got too much work to do to stand here gossiping.'

* ★ ★

Back at the Flying B, Tom traded horses, changing his saddle to a young bay but not changing the packhorse loaded with the supplies Lafe had asked him to bring from town.

'What're you up to now, son?' His father asked from the porch as Tom was tightening the cinches.

'Lafe and the boys are a little ahead of things, Pa, so I thought I'd take a ride over to the east part of the ranch. You know, I'm thinking about keeping a couple of those hands on over the winter. It's likely that we've got enough stock over there that we don't know about. What I'm thinking about is, if we do, we could be moving a bunch up onto those meadows that old man Harvey sold us. That's another thing, sometime after the winter snows clear I'd like to go up to see just what we bought.'

Asa chuckled. 'You know, it's funny when you think about it. I mean here we are, working our tails off to make up a herd to sell so as to pay off a bank note that we got so we could buy land we ain't never even seen. On the surface, that wasn't too smart, was it?'

Tom shook his head. 'But if you remember, old Harvey gave us a price for his land we couldn't turn down. And we wouldn't want anyone else living up there, would we?'

'Nope, and that was the argument you used to get me to agree. I'd sure feel better about it though if Morton was still running the bank. Some of the things Lafe says he's heard about young Sidwell don't sit too well with me.'

'Yeah, he is running things differently. But that's the way of it, don't you think? I mean look at the Flying B. Since you've been staying so close to home, I've made some changes out on the range, hiring people and firing a few of them, and things like that.'

'Maybe. So get on with your ride. How long you figure you'll be gone?'

'I figure to take enough grub for, say,

two days. I reckon that'll be enough to get an idea of what's out there and still be back in time to start the herd to the railhead.'

★ ★ ★

Looking back as he rode over a little rise Tom saw his pa was still standing on the veranda, his hands on his hips looking out over the range he'd built up.

Stopping by the gather to see how things were going, he had to smile. The hands had outdone themselves. The herd they had put together would easily bring in enough cash to pay off the loan.

'Hey, Lafe,' he called riding up to the chuck wagon. 'Got a cup of coffee for a tired rider?'

'Don't know what you'd have to be tired about, riding around like some big landowner. Did you bring me the grub I sent you for?'

Laughing, Tom tossed the packhorse's lead to the older man. 'Yeah, and then some,' he said. Swinging out of the saddle he poured a cup out of the big coffee pot sitting at the edge of the campfire. 'Those boys've been working hard. It looks like we'll be ready to start moving this bunch toward town quicker than we figured.'

'There's some good cattlemen in that crew. You still plan to go riding over eastward?'

'Uh-huh. I'll be back late tomorrow or early the next day. We can string them out and be in town before the week's out.'

'There is one thing — that young fool you hired to handle the remuda? Said his name was Jesse, don't know if'n that's his family name or his calling name. Anyway, he left. Just rode out this morning and kept riding. Didn't say anything to anyone. Was on his own horse so I reckon it don't matter much.'

'Yeah, there's no loss there. OK, I'm gone. See you tomorrow or the next day. That's when we can really get to work.' He reined away and headed up, waving to some of the other hands as he rode away from the herd.

Thinking about the horse wrangler he shook his head. Damn fool hadn't looked like much and leaving before the job was done was likely his way. Somehow he looked like that kind of man, one of those that'd never amount to much either. Ah, well, he thought, I guess the world's got all types. Least-ways he hasn't cost us anything 'cept a few meals, he told his horse.

Young Bantry might have thought differently if he saw where Jesse Earle had gone.

12

'What the hell you doing here,' Silas Sidwell snarled when the scrubby young man pushed through the banker's back door. 'You're supposed to be out there keeping an eye on the Flying B's herd.'

Sidwell sat back, his desk chair creaking. 'How's the herd look?'

'One of the better ones, I'd say. They've got a lot of top-looking beef gathered up. There'll be a pretty good payday with this bunch.'

'Stokey and his boys should be happy as bugs in a rug, then. That horse herd they took off the Davis ranch was worth more than any bank they ever robbed.'

Jesse Earle shook his head. 'Naw, that didn't turn out like everyone thought. It made old Hank madder'n hell when the buyer up in La Platte would only pay him a thousand dollars for the whole herd. Claimed the horses were too distinctive, what with their spotted rumps and all. Said they'd have to be shipped too far out of the country to sell. Said he'd have to take them clear back to Kansas before it'd be safe.'

'Well,' the banker muttered, 'he can't complain, he and that gang of his have been doing all right with the cattle they've been selling over at Ophir. Those miners will pay top price for beef.'

'Yeah, but he's not too happy about the deal you made. He says you're getting the best of it and ain't doing nothing. He thinks it's his boys what are doing all the work.'

'Now that's bull dust. But it don't matter. He's just getting ahead of himself. You tell him for me not to get greedy. The herds I point out for him are there for the taking. Without my information he and his men wouldn't know where to hit. You remind him that this is the safest money he's ever made.'

'Hey, don't yell at me,' the grimy-looking youngster said, holding up both hands, 'I'm only telling you what he said.'

Sidwell settled back, brushing at the front of his vest as if to calm himself. 'All right, it isn't your fault. But you tell him what I said. Now, when does the Flying B expect to start his drive to the railhead?'

'I dunno, the owner rode out yesterday, came into town.'

'What? Why'd he do that?'

'Came in for grub, I guess. Anyway, I came in 'cause the herd's all made up and the crew is just starting to cut out some of the younger stuff. Thought you'd want to know.'

'Yes, yes, you did the right thing,' the banker pursed his lips, thinking. 'OK, you ride on out to where Stokey's camped and tell him to be ready. I'd like to wait as long as possible before hitting the Flying B herd but he can't wait too long.'

Sidwell chuckled, 'This one's going to be the easiest one of all. It's the closest to the pass. That should make the man happy. Go on now, and don't let anyone see you. Tell him what I told you, not to get greedy and he'll continue to make money.'

'I'll tell him. Then I'm going after that damn Bantry fella. He's my meat.'

'Well you do that, but wait until after the herd's been taken, understand?'

'Yeah, I hear you.'

Riding back through the brush behind town, Jesse pulled up to look back. He'd sure like to have a drink or a restaurant meal. Shaking his head he gigged his horse on, heading over to where Stokey's camp was hidden. His brother Harlan had been part of Hank Stokey's gang from back when they were robbing miners over in the diggings. That damn fool Stokey hadn't let the youngest of the three Earle boys ride with them. Said he was too wet behind the ears. Harlan agreed. Hell, Jesse cursed silently, he's always been bossy like that.

Now, though, now that things were a little too hot for the gang over in the gold country, and now that two of the Earle brothers were dead in their graves, young Jesse was thought to be old enough.

Well, the hell with that, Jesse Earle said to himself as he rode along. I ain't about to be no more'n a messenger boy for that fool of a banker. Or for Mister Big Shot Stokey neither. No, sir. I'll tell old Stokey what the banker feller said but that's it. I'm gonna get myself that rancher what killed my brothers. Then we'll see who's too young and untested. 'C'mon, horse,' he said, jamming a spur into the horse's side. 'Rattle your hocks. Let's get this over with.'

* * *

Farther behind and riding off to one side and out of sight, Victor Garrett followed along. The bounty hunter had almost given up with his plan to watch the young kid. When he trailed him out to where a handful of cowboys were chasing cattle out of the brush, it got to be too damn hard to stay out of sight.

One night, when the fool kid snuck out of the round-up camp, he thought maybe it was finally going to be worth it, but it didn't turn out that way. All the kid had done was ride out to meet up with another rider. He got close enough to get a good look and saw it wasn't Stokey.

The two had sat in their saddles, talking for a few minutes. Garrett was too far away to make out the words. When the pair broke up their confab Garrett had followed behind the other rider. He'd lost him in the dark when the feller dropped down into a shallow ravine. Afraid to light a match when he reached the sandy bottom, Garrett couldn't tell which way the man had gone. Giving it up, he'd rolled up in his blankets thinking he'd have to turn around in the morning and go back to shadowing the fool kid. That's about all he had left. Maybe this time'd be different. After leaving the back of the bank, the young idiot hadn't taken off for the round-up holding ground like

Garrett had expected but had ridden more eastward. Maybe he was at last going to lead the manhunter to the outlaw boss.

Keeping one eye on the horseman he was behind, Garrett checked the loads, first in his saddle carbine and then in the Colt .44 he carried high up on one hip.

★   ★   ★

It had been a couple years since Tom Bantry had ridden out to the far eastern section of the Flying B. His pa had staked it out when he first set out his boundaries, taking in a lot more land that he thought he'd need or even easily work rather than too little. At that time the government was allowing home-steaders a section, 640 acres, free. All they had to do was prove up on it. That wasn't enough for any cattle man to be able to raise a profitable herd. Rather than argue with that same government that it took a lot more than a single section, most men just bought the land they wanted from the railroad.

At that time, with sufficient flat bottom land, neither Asa Bantry nor Lafe Gunnison, his right-hand man, had bothered to look farther up in the high country. Well, Tom smiled to himself, that didn't matter any more. Once the herd was delivered and the loan paid off, he'd take a ride up there to see what that old trapper had sold them.

The country he was riding through was a little higher than the land the rest of the ranch was on. Standing tall in the saddle, all he could see was a series of rolling slopes, from here to the beginning of the mountain range, each covered with good, sun-dried summer grass. Scanning the distant range while giving his horse a blow, he could see how the land tilted upwards for another five miles or so before the grassland turned into brush. Above that, the blue curtain of a pine forest indicated where the bottom edge of the eastern rim of the upper basin was. Far to the left the rocky bluff that looked impassable stood tall and sheer in the early afternoon sunshine. It wasn't obvious but according to old Leander Harvey there was a good route along the near side of that outcropping that climbed in easy stages up to a meadow. Another, larger piece of grazing land just a bit west of that was a little higher. The grass up there, the trapper'd said, was sweet and well-watered. Snow covered it in the deep of winter, of course, but not so bad a herd couldn't make it. Lots of protection along the northern side, he'd explained, drawing a rough map on a piece of butcher paper.

Looking ahead to the mountains in front of him, Tom smiled.

'You know, horse,' he murmured to the bay, 'I'll bet there's some good deer hunting to be had up in those trees. We'll have to remember and come up after the first snow fall.'

The horse didn't say anything, just reached down to chomp at a clump of prairie grass.

Kneeing his mount forward, Tom kept the horse at a gentle trot, his eyes sweeping the tall grass, keeping a watch for livestock. He'd noticed small bunches scattered here and there but nothing like what was feeding down on the flats. Since leaving the lowlands he had seen how the number of cattle had thinned out. The grass might be good but there was more accessible water down below. Come spring, he thought, he'd put a crew up here to roust out as many head as possible then send the older stock to market.

Thinking about the possibility of a hunting trip, he thought he'd ride on up to the tree line to give it all a closer look.

An hour or so later he was surprised to come upon sign that a small bunch of cattle had been driven across the upper range. Puzzled, he backtracked the wide swath of prints left by the animals. From the sign, he figured there had been no more than four or five men pushing them along and they hadn't

145

been in any hurry, letting the cattle graze as they ambled.

Climbing down out of the saddle he kicked at a pile of cow dung, seeing how dry it was. More than likely, he figured, the drive had passed by here more than a couple weeks before. Crouching over a spot where a horse had stepped clear of the mess left by the cattle, he studied the hoof prints. Cursing under his breath at not being able to find some mark that could help identify who the rider was, he stood up to find himself staring at a group of men sitting their saddles, watching him. Each one, he noted, was holding a rifle or pistol and were all pointed at him.

'Well, hello,' he said, standing still and being careful to keep his hand away from his belt gun. 'Guess I wasn't paying close enough attention. Didn't hear you come up.'

'Doesn't matter,' one man said, sitting his horse a little ahead of the others. Obviously he was their leader. 'We been watching you and was waiting to see what you'd do when you come across that trail.'

Tom nodded. 'And now you've seen it, haven't you. How about telling that little army you got behind you to point those weapons somewhere else?'

'Not until we know what the hell you think you're doing.'

Looking over the mounted men, one at a time, Tom frowned. Of the seven men he thought he'd seen a couple before, likely in town, but he didn't know the names of any of them.

'Nope,' he said, looking back at the man asking the questions. 'It doesn't work that way. This is Flying B range you're on and I'm Flying B. So how about you explaining why you're on my land and pointing half a dozen gun barrels at me.'

'Hey, Mr Davis,' said a younger man farther back, 'I seen him in town once or twice. That's Tom Bantry. It's his old man that owns the Flying B ranch, all right.'

Davis didn't move, keeping his eyes

focused on Tom and his rifle centered on Tom's chest. 'I know who he is but it don't mean he doesn't know about the rustling. Now, Mister Bantry, let's hear from you. What the hell you doing out here.'

Glancing at the horse Davis was riding, he figured the man had to be Horace Davis. The spotted rump was a sure sign of an Appaloosa.

'If I were to come barreling across one of your horse pastures, pointing my Henry at you, how quick would you be calling out a welcome? As I said, Horace Davis, you're on my land so I'll ask the questions.'

Davis hesitated a bit before raising his rifle until the stock was resting on his thigh, the barrel aiming at the sky. 'How'd you know who I was?'

'Riding a spotted rumped horse? Use your head, old man. Now I'm getting mighty uncomfortable about this, so tell those fools you got behind you to point them guns somewhere else or start shooting.' Tom smiled coldly, slowly letting his right hand ease down toward the butt of his holstered Colt, thumbing the thong off the Colt's hammer.

'Hey, Mr Davis,' the same feller said, 'he's right. We got no call to be pressuring him. Mister Bantry,' he called a little louder, 'don't go shooting. I'm moving aside now.'

Out of the corner of his eye Tom saw one and then the other of the men edge their mounts to either side leaving the Appaloosa and Tom facing each other.

'You got something to add to this, Davis?' asked Tom, his voice now hard.

'Damn you. Someone stole my horses. Cost me my ranch. It's the same bunch of thieves that's been stealing cattle down in the southern end of the basin. Now we ride up here, following the trail left by one herd of rustled stock and what do we find? You. And I know you're a great friend of that crooked banker, Sidwell. And guess what, that trail goes right across land the banker's partner says is his. And he won't tell us what he's doing. That makes me damn suspicious.'

For a long moment nobody moved or said anything.

'OK, Davis, you've had your say. Now here's mine: go to hell! You've all but called me a thief and a rustler. You're angry, and like a rabid dog you're ready to bite anyone and everyone. Well,' Tom continued, his voice low and hard, 'go ahead, you got one chance. You go to dropping the barrel of that long gun my way and I'm going to pull iron. You might just get a slug in me but believe it, you'll die.'

13

Watching the horseman's eyes, Tom let
a little smile lift his lips. The slight
breeze he felt against the hair on his
neck almost tickled. Not the kind of
thing he wanted to be thinking about
when he might be dead in a minute.
The only sound was that of the air
moving through the tall, sun-baked
grass as the two men, one standing and
the other sitting comfortably in his
saddle, stared at each other.

'You fools,' one of the riders
snarled disgustedly and reined his
horse to stand between them. 'One of
you is acting like a spoiled child and
the other, well, I don't know what.
Now, you want to start shooting, go
ahead. It'll be me and my horse that
gets it. That'll answer everything,
won't it.'

'Get out of the way, Lew,' Davis

yelled, using his knees to make his horse side step.

Lew nudged his horse, keeping in front of the angry man. 'Sure, so you can go on acting the fool. Like the man says, he's got a right to be here, it's his range. You're out of line and none of us is gonna be a part of it. This isn't why we're out here. Settle down,' he ordered.

'How come nobody's hit his range?' yelled Davis, sounding weak and whiny. Tom saw that the man's frustration limit had been reached. 'Tell me that, will you. Damn it, I've lost everything and the rustlers have left him alone. It's clear to me; he's got to be part of it, him and that damn banker friend of his.'

With neither man paying any attention to him, Tom let his body relax and climbed back onto his horse.

Lew was still sitting between them. 'You're not making any sense, Davis. All the rustling has been to the south end of the basin. I don't know why, nobody except the rustlers do. That don't mean the ranchers up here are behind it all. That don't make any sense at all and you'd know it, if you stopped to think.'

'Christ, whose side are you on, Lew?' Davis snarled feebly, then gaining strength he pointed at the mounted man with his left hand. 'Hey, come to think on it, you haven't lost any stock either.'

'Well, the hell with it,' Lew said, disgust thick in his words, 'I'm going home. Davis, you're on your own.'

Heeling his horse, Lew rode around the Appaloosa and followed by the rest of the horsemen, rode back the way they'd come. Davis and Tom could have been two riders, stopping to share a smoke and a bit of gossip, but neither was talking.

'Ah, Christ,' Davis said finally, shoving his rifle back in the scabbard. 'I still think there's something not right about this but Lew is right. I haven't been thinking right since being chased off my spread. I ain't apologizing, mind you,' he went on, taking out a faded bandanna and wiping the inside of his wide-brimmed hat, 'but I can't simply shoot you either.'

Tom slouched in the leather. 'I heard Buford Sullivan say you and your wife were the kind of people the basin needs. Old Buford is my friend too, you know. There's nothing I can do about what Silas Sidwell's been doing, but if you think you got dealt with unfairly or illegally I'd suggest you contact the sheriff up in La Platte, or the state government down in the capital. I heard that a judge had to sign off on the foreclosure so maybe there's nothing that can be done, but riding around wanting to shoot people certainly isn't the way. Think of your wife. What'll she do if you get hanged for murder.'

Shaking his head, Davis turned his horse and silently rode away, following the tracks left by Lew and the others.

For a long moment Tom watched him, feeling the sweat on his back cool wondering how he'd feel if he lost the Flying B.

154

14

Hank Stokey was a stoop-shouldered man looking older than his years. A rider of the owlhoot trail since a boy he'd never been in on a big score. The closest he'd ever come was when riding with Henry Starr. At the time Starr was like a god for the young Stokey and that was when he learned all he knew about robbing banks. When Starr was caught down in West Texas, Stokey got away and rode north. He might have had the famous Starr as a mentor but he apparently didn't learn enough. Like most outlaws riding the back trails, Stokey never earned as much as any forty-a-month cowpoke.

Feeling the aches and pains of his rough life, Stokey had thought he'd at last found his reward in the Ophir gold district. For almost a year he and a handful of followers controlled the trails coming out of that area. When the miners' committee got too well organized he went looking for new ranges to ride, getting out just in time, if that last ambush was any sign.

'OK, so that fool of a banker wants us to hit the Flying B,' he mused after hearing what young Jesse Earle had to tell him. 'What the hell does he mean 'Soon but not just yet'? He don't know nothing.' Looking around the campfire at the other men, he spit into the coals. 'We'll hit it when I say we will. But damme, I still don't like it. Working for some banker ain't something I like. I'll tell you, this one's going to be the last one, boys, and we just might teach that fool a lesson when we ride out.'

Along with young Earle, three other riders had been siding Hank Stokey in this rustling operation. Dwight Curry, who liked it when they called him Kid Curry, was a jug-eared man of about twenty or so. Skinny from never getting enough to eat when growing up, he was always hungry. While Stokey was talking, Curry was chewing on a half-rotten apple he'd found somewhere.

Pie-eyed Wilson was the oldest of the gang and had only been riding with these boys a few weeks. Nobody trusted Wilson, mainly because you could never tell which eye was looking at you.

The third member was part Indian, Half-breed Charlie. The son of a San Antonio Mexican whore and any one of a dozen men, Charlie had learned early in life that if people thought he was a Redskin they'd leave him alone. Probably afraid he'd go on the warpath and scalp someone. Nobody was ever afraid of a Mexican. Charlie liked the idea of getting out of the basin.

Somehow he felt there was a lot of danger for him in this part of the country. He had been thought of as being half-Indian so long that he actually believed it was his Indian spirit guide that was warning him.

Stokey grimaced, thinking about his crew. There had been other men at various times. For a while Harlan Earle, young Jesse's brother, had been part of things. Hell, even the other Earle, Rufus, had ridden with Stokey once. That Earle wasn't all there in the head, the outlaw boss thought, and wasn't too unhappy when Harlan had sent him off somewhere.

He was glad when Harlan had ridden out, too. Leading a bunch of lazy, not too smart, gun-happy saddle-bums was hard enough as it was without having to worry about someone who thought too much of himself. Too bad about his getting killed down there in town, though. Now he was stuck with Jesse Earle who took after his older brother, thinking he could do better. Shaking his head, Stokey wanted to scream over his bad luck. It'd always been that way, he cursed silently, never able to get anyone good to ride with him.

'Yeah, all right then, Earle. We all know what the banker wants, now tell me, how long you figure it'll be until the Flying B herd hits the trail?'

Earle glowed. At last Hank Stokey was after his help. 'Any day, now. They only wanted about a hundred head and they got that yesterday. I thought they'd wait until Bantry came back; he went riding out yesterday before noon. Or so I heard. I don't know if'n they'll wait for him or not.'

'Uh-huh. How many men're we likely to find making the drive?'

'There's only been six putting the herd together.'

'Well, how many do you figure will be on the trail? All six?'

'Hells bells, I dunno.'

Stokey spit his tobacco into the fire and cussed. 'What the hell good are ya, then?' His reaction crushed Earle. 'Well, it don't matter. We'll go take a look-see in the morning.'

Turning away, the outlaw boss threw himself down on his bedroll and pulled the cork from a bottle of whiskey.

★　★　★

A quarter-mile away, sitting in front of a large patch of sagebrush, Victor Garrett watched the camp with a pair of binoculars. Some time in the past he'd traded a sway-backed horse for the binoculars which had been stripped from a dead Reb during the last few days of the Great War. Garrett didn't know that and wouldn't have cared if he did.

He'd followed the young rider from the back door of the bank, feeling better about it when the skinny youth rode off to the north-east and not back toward the Flying B. It was the smell of smoke that brought him to leave off the rider's trail. Shielded by the sagebrush he studied the men hunkered around the fire. From this distance he couldn't decide which one was Stokey. The outlaw leader had been described to him but from where he was sitting he couldn't tell which one of the men down there it'd be. Not wanting to miss out he decided to wait to see what they were going to do.

Wrapped up in his bedding, he settled in, chewing pieces of dried beef strips for his supper. Maybe tomorrow, he thought. This would all be over tomorrow if he could get his shot at Hank Stokey.

15

Tom Bantry gave up the idea of riding up into the forests and followed the trail left by the cattle. Throughout the afternoon he kept his horse at a comfortable trot, eating up the country-side. The tracks left by the herd slowly angled upwards and he figured the drivers were using the rocky bluff as their goal. That reckoning proved right. As the sun was settling behind the high mountain range far beyond the bluff he saw the beginning of what had to be the way up into the upland meadows that Leander Harvey had talked about. The rustlers were using that high pass over the mountains.

Watering his horse at a small rivulet of water falling from a spring higher up Tom decided to give up the trail and make camp. He'd think about it and in the morning settle on whether to pursue the herd or go back to turn what he'd found over to Sullivan.

Making a meal of food from his saddle-bags, boiling up the last of his coffee over a small fire, he settled with his back against a fallen tree trunk to watch the night come on over the range below. The main buildings of the Flying B were too far away for any lights to be seen but the view was worth studying in the growing dark.

The night sky was a dusky gray when the first star showed itself just above the eastern horizon. Relaxed and sipping the cooling coffee, Tom tensed as he caught a flash of movement just below where he sat. Not moving he watched as a thin-bodied coyote crept slowly from behind a clump of prairie grass. Freezing momentarily before jumping onto whatever kind of rodent it had been stalking, the coyote made its kill.

That was what was likely to happen to him, he decided, if he were to go on following the herd. It had to be rustled livestock he'd been following. Even if the trail was cold that was no guarantee that the herd had been moved on. The rustlers hadn't looked to be pushing the stolen stock any. With nobody around up in the high country it could be the cattle were being held up in one of the meadows to fatten before being moved on. If that was the case, then it'd be most likely the rustlers would be watching their back trail. Turning into his bedroll he smiled. The rodents he'd been following wouldn't get to jump him. Following on up the trail would be left to someone else.

★ ★ ★

The ride down from the bluff seemed quick and it was only a little past midday when Tom rode into the Flying B yard. Stripping the leather from his horse, he gave the animal a well-earned currying before roping a fresh mount. Dropping the reins over the porch railing he went in to talk with his father.

'Hey, didn't know you was back,' Asa

Bantry called as Tom pushed through the front door. 'Learn anything from your little jaunt out to the east range? Come on out to the kitchen. There's a fresh pot of coffee on the stove.'

Once the two men had settled around the big wooden table with steaming cups in front of them he asked the question, 'What'd you find out there?'

'It's good country, Pa. A little higher and not as much water but there's good grass and enough livestock to make a sweep worthwhile. I figure we could bring out the older beeves to send to market next spring and keep the young stuff to mature. No, it was something else I found that's interesting,' and he went on to tell the older man about the rustlers' use of the high meadows.

'Damme, son, you did the right thing, not following them outlaws. But you know, that makes me wonder about Old Harvey. We'd heard that the rustlers were working the southern end of the basin some time before he came down to make us the offer for that land. I wonder if he didn't know they were moving the stolen stock up over the pass and wanted to get out. What do you figure?'

Tom frowned. 'Well, we don't know much about that old man, now do we. But does it matter? All that up there is paid for and registered with the land office over in La Platte. Maybe that's why he wanted to sell, to get away from being part of it if someone caught up with the cattle thieves or maybe not. I'm thinking about riding in and talking to Buford about the pass being used. I guess it won't matter to anyone to bring the old man into it. As far as the rustlers go, I say we leave it up to our deputy to notify the law up in La Platte.'

'Good thinking.'

'I'll stop by and see how the gather is coming before I ride on into town.'

* * *

With a quick meal under his belt and riding a fresh mount, Tom rode out to the holding ground. Coming over the low ridge and looking down at the work going on, he saw that the herd would have to start moving; the grass in the little valley was about all gone.

'Well,' Lafe called from the back of the chuckwagon as he rode in, 'did you come back to work or just to sit there on that buckskin and watch others do the job?'

Tom laughed and sitting back in the saddle nodded. 'Yeah, that's about right. I'm going on into town and thought I'd stop and see how you're getting along.'

'Harrumph,' the older man snorted, 'now if that doesn't sound like I figured, I don't know what would. Well, we're ready to get these critters to walking. They're eating us out of grass and the crew has about emptied the chuckwagon. I figure we'll head them out early in the morning. That'll put us at the rail yard in about four or five days' time. How's that sound?'

Tom thought a moment. This was the first day of the month and the bank note was due on the tenth. That would leave plenty of time.

'Sounds good to me. I've got to go talk with the deputy sheriff. Tell you what, to make up for leaving all the work to you, I'll volunteer to ride drag when I get back. How's that sound?'

'Well, don't that beat all. You make a great promise like that knowing if'n you ride now you won't get to town before midday tomorrow. It'll be the day after that before you can get back. We'll have a day or even a day and a half on the trail by then. Those critters'll be all settled in and riding drag won't be so bad. What a great offer, you're making.'

'Hmm,' Tom frowned with a little smile playing on his lips. 'You know, I never thought of it that way,' he said, chuckling. 'Oh, well, it's the thought that counts, isn't it?'

Lafe could only snigger. 'I guess.'

Getting serious, he put a rope-scarred

old hand on the buckskin's shoulder and looked up at the younger man. 'You know, there're some good men in that crew you hired. They've been working damn hard.'

'Good. You don't need to say anything but I'm thinking about keeping one or two on over winter. Maybe start to move some of the cattle I found up on the east range a little early. We'll see.'

* * *

Getting to town the next day in time for a midday meal, Tom first left his buckskin off at the livery before heading for the Mexican's café. The chances were good, he figured, he'd find Buford sitting there drinking coffee. He was right.

Pushing through the restaurant door he almost stopped to savor the wonderful smells coming from whatever was on the stove.

'Hey, there, Buford,' he called, seeing

the deputy sheriff sitting with Silas Sidwell at a table in back, 'is this where you spend all your time? And what does that bride of yours think of the company you're hanging out with. Hiyah, Silas,' he added.

Sullivan laughed and pointed to an empty chair. 'Well, look what the cat dragged in. Come sit down and tell us what devilment you've been up to.'

Smiling, Silas pushed the chair out from the table for Tom.

'Oh, not much,' the cowboy sighed as he relaxed. 'You know how it is, just getting a herd ready to bring into the yards.' Glancing over at the banker he remembered his run-in with Davis. 'I wouldn't want to be late with paying off that little note I took out with the bank, now would I?'

'Ah, well, Tom, I can't see how that could happen,' Silas said softly. 'Well, as much as I'd like to, I can't be setting here when there's work back at the bank to do. I'll catch up with the both of you later.'

The two men watched the banker pay his bill and go out the door.

Sullivan sighed. 'You know, he's sure different since his pa died. Never has time to sit and talk or to go have a drink at the Past Time or anything.'

'I had a run-in with that horse rancher Davis while I was out riding our east range,' said Tom softly. 'He's hurting over losing his spread and blames it all on Silas. I told him if he thought he'd been done wrong to take it to the law. Has he said anything to you about it?'

'No, but it's clear that it's eating him up. Now, how's the herd coming along?'

'Good. Lafe said he planned on having them moving down toward the loading pens today. That's the good news. The better news is while riding that far range I came across what looked like the trail of a small jag of cattle being driven. Way it looks, there were four, maybe five riders pushing fifty or sixty head west across our upper

171

range. I followed them to where they headed up into the high country. Did you know there's a series of meadows up there?'

Sullivan shook his head.

'Well, there are. And if you go far enough you'll find a pass through those mountains, too. I don't know exactly where it leads but that'd be getting close to the Ophir district, wouldn't it?'

'Yeah,' Sullivan said slowly, 'that's the right direction for Ophir anyhow. What are you thinking it's all about — the rustling that's been going on?'

'Uh-huh. Maybe the cattle that left that sign came from some spread up this way and anything taken down south was run that way, I don't know. But it's clear that at least one herd's been run up into the high country. Nobody ever rides up there so it'd be perfect for getting stolen stock out of the northern end of the basin. I figured to let you know so you could notify the sheriff's office up at the county seat. My herd should be at the yard in another four or five days and then I can lead a posse up to that trail if you want.'

'I'll wire the sheriff and tell him first thing in the morning. This may be just what he's needed to bring an end to it. Now, let me tell you my good news.' He waited a beat before going on. 'Mattie's gotten Cora to talking.'

Tom was surprised at how good that news made him feel.

'Of course,' the lawman went on, 'the young woman isn't saying much and she shuts right down as soon as I walk into the house, but Mattie says each day she seems a little calmer and talks a little more. Now, that is good to hear, isn't it?'

Tom nodded. 'Yeah, that's good. I wonder what made her change.'

'Mattie thinks it's because she feels safe. Doing things a woman does, whether it's cooking or sewing or the like is calming, she says, and maybe that's what Cora needs. Oh, and Bobby has stopped fighting his going to school. He seems to think you promised to take him fishing if he did whatever Mattie and Cora told him to do. Is that what happened?'

Trying to remember what he'd told the boy, Tom could only nod. 'I might have said something like that. I guess a fishing trip wouldn't be too hard to do. Oh, and while on that subject, I may have found where we ought to go deer hunting, too. We'll have to talk about it, but right now I'm heading for the hotel. I've got to get back to the herd as early as I can tomorrow to help with the drive. Boy, I'll be damn glad when that's done with.'

16

Garrett catnapped through the night, coming awake every so often to scan the outlaw camp below, not getting any real rest but afraid Stokey and his boys would ride out before he got his shot. He hadn't been able to get close enough to make out which was the man he wanted so that's about all he could do.

He needn't have worried. The five men made enough noise to wake the dead getting the morning fire going and saddling up their horses. Even the smell of coffee being brewed came strongly to him, being carried on an early morning breeze from the little low spot the camp was in up to where the manhunter watched. Chewing the last of his stale, dried beef jerky, he grimaced.

Waiting to see which way they would be riding, he quickly led his horse to a clump of trees to one side when it looked like they were heading his way. Holding his horse's nose so it wouldn't snort, he watched as the riders rode by. Even coming as close as they did, he couldn't tell from the way they were bunched which one would be the leader. The only one he recognized was the Earle kid.

Once again, careful to keep out of sight, he followed along.

At first he thought they would be heading south toward Ferris Corners. That didn't seem likely. He couldn't think of why they'd want to go and do that. Reaching the flat rolling country, he dropped back, putting a little more distance between them as the group of horsemen, now not so tightly bunched, angled a little more westward. Riding so purposefully, he figured they were about to take some poor rancher's livestock.

Keeping a steady pace he worked to remain far enough back so they wouldn't spot him but still not lose them. The morning sun was high overhead when, coming up on a slight rise, he pulled up. The gang was bunched, all facing something ahead, clearly talking. One of the men, he noted was giving directions, waving an arm first one way and then the other. This would have to be Stokey.

Quickly reaching for his binoculars, he studied the outlaws, marking which one was his target. The one giving orders was not the biggest of the gang, but the only one wearing a worn sheepskin vest, the kind with the wool outside, over a faded red shirt. The man's sloping shoulders also set him apart. Victor Garrett, sitting back, relaxed. He knew his man at last.

Separating, Stokey's crew rode out, circling around whatever was just below where they had been, leaving their boss sitting, obviously waiting.

From Garrett's vantage point, he wasn't able to see exactly what they were doing but understanding the kind of men they were he wasn't surprised to hear faint gunfire just before the man slouching in the saddle sunk the spurs to his mount. Waving a long-barreled handgun, the outlaw chief charged out of sight.

Hurrying to where he could see, Garrett then reined back, halting his horse just below the top of a low ridge. The sound of gunfire, yelling men and bawling cattle came rushing up to him. Through a thick cloud of dust he could just barely make out a small herd of cattle milling around, close to stampeding down in the bottom of a small hollow. Riders in as much confusion were scattered around the edges of the herd. One or two, he saw were firing at others. From where he sat it was impossible to tell who was being attacked. As he watched, one man, his body flopping loosely, fell from the back of a running horse. A canvas-covered wagon sat still off to one side, its team of horses rearing in the harness.

Garrett lost track of what was happening down below when his horse started fighting the bit and he wasn't sure whether the animal wanted to get in on the action or simply wanted to escape. Dropping back away from the battle, he secured his horse to a sturdy bush and hurried back up the rise to see what was happening. Lying on his stomach he watched, hoping his man wasn't one of those lying motionless in the dirt. This wasn't his fight and even if it was, there was nothing he could do. The herd would be taken by the rustlers.

The fact was, he thought, watching the action below, this could work in his favor. A herd, even a small one like this, could work in his best interests. To drive the cattle anywhere, the thieves would have to spread out. Saving the cattle wasn't in his plans, but collecting on the outlaw leader, dead or alive, was.

* * *

The attack came as a complete surprise to the Flying B hands, who had been concentrating on getting the hundred or so head started on the drive out of the holding area. Lafe had swung the chuckwagon far to one side in order to move up alongside the cattle to get ahead of them as they were strung out. When he heard the first shots he cursed thinking one of the men had likely thought to get the cows moving by shooting over their heads. Glancing back to see who could be so foolish, he spotted a stranger, riding hell-bent for leather in his direction, waving a six-gun.

'What the hell's going on,' he yelled, reaching at the same time for the rifle on the floorboards at his feet. 'It's damn rustlers,' he said quietly as he levered a shell into the breach, brought it up and without aiming shot at the rider, missing. Before he could work the lever a second time, he was slammed back, dropping the weapon and falling off the wagon seat.

The rider, Half-breed Charlie, gave out his version of a war-cry and charged past without taking a second look. The draft horses pulling the wagon felt the reins go slack and lumbered to a halt. One of the big dapple-gray Percherons, catching the scent of blood, panicked and tried to bolt but was held back by the other, older draft horse.

To Billy Horton the battle started when he saw a stranger gallop across in front of the herd. Billy was riding along one side of the herd, slowly using his horse to start a few head moving by pushing at them. Reining back in surprise, he cursed.

'What do you think you're doing?' he yelled and then ducked low when he saw the handgun pointed at him. Jabbing a spur into the side of his horse, he neck-reined the animal away, running square into the side of a slow-moving cow.

The horse faltered, trying to regain its balance, but ended up swerving abruptly, tossing the cowboy out of the saddle. Landing on his back in the dirt,

Horton instinctively rolled away from the thrashing hoofs. The little jag of beeves he'd been working panicked into a run, fleeing away from the pitching horse.

On his feet, Horton pulled his Colt and angrily tried to find the damn fool who'd shot at him. That man had disappeared in the cloud of dust churned up by the stampeding cattle. Knowing he was in a bad place to be and seeing his horse, its reins dragging, he scrambled over grabbing at the strips of leather. Swinging into the saddle, still with his revolver in hand he jumped the horse away from the disordered herd.

Seeing another strange rider, this one using a rifle, Horton snapped a shot. His horse, still not totally under control, bolted at that moment, making Horton miss. He didn't see where the bullet came from but felt his horse shudder as it was hit. Kicking loose from the stirrups, the cowboy tried to hang on to his weapon as he jumped free. Hitting the ground on one shoulder he rolled, his head slamming into the ground. Feeling his Colt fall from his hand, the last thing he saw was a stranger pointing a rifle at his head. The jolt of being hit was the last thing he was aware of as he lost consciousness.

The fight lasted only a few minutes. When the last of the herders were out of the battle the rustlers started riding around the cattle. Working as a unit, they forced the animals into a near solid mass. When one old mosey horned bull saw what looked like a way out, bellowing loudly, it lunged up and out of the shallow holding ground. The rest of the bunch, running with fear, followed and within minutes the cattle were strung out, the old bull in front leading the way, not toward the loading pens at the railyard but west, toward the mountains.

17

Sleeping in a bed after spending so many nights on the ground felt good and Tom took advantage of it, not getting up until the street below was filled with sunlight. Breakfast at the Mexican's, a hot bath at the Chinese laundry, a shave at Curley's and he felt like a new man.

He'd given the idea of stopping by Mattie Andrews's house some thought but decided it'd be better if he passed that up. 'Don't want anyone to start thinking I've got too big an interest in that girl, Cora Lee,' he thought as he cinched up the saddle on the buckskin, then quickly correcting himself, 'a woman, not a girl'. Smiling at the memory of her in the snug-topped dress, he nodded. 'Nope, certainly not a girl.'

Feeling extra good about things, he

almost broke out in song as he rode out of town, but didn't, not knowing how the buckskin would react to the noise.

Keeping the horse at a steady pace, he figured to meet up with the herd sometime before dark. Not wanting to waste time, he stopped only briefly for a noontime meal, not taking time to brew coffee but washing down the sandwich he'd had packed back in town with clear spring water. Starting to worry a little when by the time the sun was ducking behind the far mountains he hadn't seen any sign of the herd, he touched a spur to the horse's flank.

Galloping into the dusk ate up the miles but by full dark he still hadn't been anything of his cattle.

'Well,' he muttered to the sweat covered buckskin, 'maybe they weren't ready to move as soon as Lafe figured. Yeah,' he went on a short time later, 'that's probably what happened.' Pulling back on the reins, he slowed the horse to a walk, letting the animal cool down.

'Guess it's back to the bedroll and rocky ground tonight, old feller. Leastways I'll have a good cup of coffee with my beef jerky.'

Up before dawn, he quickly heated the left-over coffee and was in the saddle as the false dawn outlined the eastern horizon. The buckskin had rolled and rested and now seemed to want to run. Tom let it, standing tall in the stirrups when, coming up on a rise, he hoped to see the herd strung out ahead.

The sight greeting him as he stopped to look down into the little swale that had been used to hold the herd twisted his stomach into a knot. The valley was empty.

Sitting back in the leather he studied the grassland below. It was clear that the herd had been there, most of the grass was gone leaving only bare brown dirt behind. A blackened mound of ashes marked where the big campfire had been and from where he sat he could just make out the twin ruts made by the chuckwagon. There wasn't a sign of the cattle.

Swinging his mount around, he sent the buckskin racing toward the ranch headquarters.

★   ★   ★

From a mile or so away he saw the canvas top of the chuckwagon sitting in front of the main house. His horse was thick with foam, its breath coming in deep, raspy gulps. Stripping the rigging from the animal, he turned it into the nearest corral before running up the steps and busting through the front door.

'What the — ' his pa yelled, jumping from where he'd been crouching on the floor in front of the horse-hair covered sofa. A blanket-covered body was lying still on the couch.

'Pa, what the hell happened,' Tom bawled out, not stopping until he stood looking down at Lafe's pale, unmoving face. 'Is he dead?'

'No, boy, he's sleeping. Took a bullet in the shoulder, high up. Lost a lot of blood before anyone could get the bleeding stopped. He's been sleeping since they brought him in yesterday afternoon.'

'What the hell happened?'

'Rustlers hit the herd. That feller you hired, Horton? He brought Lafe in, in the back of the grub wagon. The other hands didn't make it. Horton said nobody saw the rustlers come in on them. Just turned up suddenly and started shooting. Figured there was four or five of them. The herd had just gotten strung out when the bustards hit, according to Horton. Caught the men all spread out and surprised them. He said Lafe got off a couple shots from his seat on the wagon before being hit.'

'Lafe and Horton the only ones alive?'

'Yeah. He wrapped the others in their blankets and tied them to the back of a couple horses. Brought them all in.

They're over in the barn. Horton's horse was shot out from under him and one of the rustlers came up and shot him before he could get up. Blew a hole in his hat and cut a crease in his scalp. They'd gone when he regained consciousness. Not a cow in sight.'

'Damn, Pa. I should have been there instead of going into town.'

'Probably best you weren't or it'd be you laying in your blankets over in the hay.'

'Where's Horton now?'

'He blacked out after helping me get Lafe in the house. I put him in your bed — hope you don't mind. He's been mostly sleeping. Last time I looked in I saw he was running a fever and having troublesome dreams. Nightmares, I'd say. Probably reliving the shooting.'

'Pa, we got to get those beeves back. That note with Silas comes due in less than two weeks and those cattle are going to pay it off.' Striding over to the glass-fronted gun cabinet, he pulled open a drawer below the half-dozen rifles and shotguns. Taking a box of .44 caliber shells he filled the pockets of the jacket he was wearing.

'What are you going to do, boy?' asked the elder Bantry, knowing before he opened his mouth.

'Only thing I can do, Pa. Going in to report this to Buford won't do it, and riding up to the sheriff's office would be the same. If it's going to get done, it's going to be me that does it.'

'Ah, Tom, can't you go talk to Silas? Get an extension on the loan? He's always been a good friend of yours.'

Tom shook his head. 'Silas has changed, Pa. I can just see him turning me down saying he's got to treat everyone the same. He's just not the same person I grew up with.'

'Well, you make sure you come back, you hear? I don't want to have to run this place by myself.'

Tom nodded and with a last glance down at Lafe, went outside to saddle a fresh mount.

Thinking he'd take up the trail left

behind by the rustlers, Tom rode hard for a few minutes before pulling his horse to a halt. Why ride clear back to the little valley when he had a pretty good idea where the herd was being driven, up into the high meadows and then over the pass. Changing direction, he turned west toward the mountains, holding the horse to a trot.

Riding easy in the saddle he started thinking about what he'd do when he caught up with the thieves. With only his Henry and the holstered Colt to back up his play, he tried to come up with a plan.

'Well, horse,' he said after a while, stopping to give the animal a chance to blow, 'I'd feel a lot better if Billy Horton was riding with me. Him or anyone else, for that matter. Guess we'll just have to see how things work out and try to take advantage of what we find.'

18

Half-breed Charlie was damn mad. As always he'd done his part, shooting and yelling, but just like always here he was riding drag, eating the dust of the herd of stolen cattle. He didn't pay any notice that Jesse Earle had also been sent to the back of the herd.

That damn Stokey, Charlie thought for the hundredth time, he'll get his one of these days. Maybe it's time to cut loose from this pack, his thoughts went on as he kneed his horse over to one side to push a straggler back into the bunch. It'd been all right when they were stealing gold from the miners over in the mining district, but running livestock was work.

Hank Stokey riding a quarter-mile ahead was feeling pretty good. They'd taken the herd with none of his men taking a bullet and now, even with their horses starting to tire, they were making good time. Feeling his horse, a dun-colored mustang, stumble he turned back. The chances of anyone coming up behind them today were slight and another day would see them climbing out of the flat land. They'd be safe up there.

'Hey,' he called to Curry, waving a hand in a circular motion high over his head, 'wheel them around. This is as good a place as any to spend the night.'

'Ain't no water I can see,' the young outlaw griped, stopping his horse alongside Stokey's mustang.

'Damn it, do what I tell you. Water don't matter. We got enough for ourselves and it'll make it easier getting these critters moving come sunup. There's a little creek a couple miles ahead and once we get them going they'll smell it. Now,' he waved a hand, dismissing the complaint, 'turn those leaders in a tight circle. Go on.'

Standing high in the stirrups, he waved his intentions to the rider riding on the far side, Wilson.

Once the herd had settled, a small fire was lit and the camp coffee pot set to boil. No one questioned their boss when he called out the night riding schedule. Charlie carefully kept his cold black eyes on the ground when he heard he'd been given the midnight trick. Yeah, he swore silently, not letting Stokey see his anger, sooner or later, boss, sooner or later.

*　*　*

Garrett had no trouble now, keeping Stokey and his men in sight. Once the cattle got over their scare they settled down, moving along at a slow but steady pace. From a slight rise the manhunter used his binoculars and scanned the forest-covered mountain range that contained this end of the basin, trying to see where the rustlers were taking the herd. From the direction they were being pushed, he figured there must be a way through that barrier. He just couldn't see it from where he was. Keeping out of sight he dropped down, sure he wouldn't lose contact with Stokey now.

The sun was getting near that western range when he spotted the thin spiral of smoke in the still air. It'd been a warm day, with only a light scattering of fluffy clouds hanging in the blue sky. For a while, earlier on, a gentle breeze had rustled the tops of the grasses but that had died as evening came on. The smoke had to be the outlaws' camp.

Shaking his Confederate Army tin canteen he didn't think he had enough water for coffee. Somewhere ahead there would have to be water. The cattle would have to be watered before long. Garrett kneed his horse to the side and made a wide circle around the outlaw camp.

*   *   *

Tom had kept his horse at a mile-eating trot, keeping its head higher than

195

normal in the belief that it would make the animal's breathing easier. Even so, he got down and led it at times to give it a chance to blow.

He didn't know it but the creek he made his camp beside just about dusk was the same one Victor Garrett had dropped his bedroll beside. The two men were about five miles apart. They couldn't know that soon one of them would be saving the life of the other.

★   ★   ★

Stokey had the herd moving as the sun came up over the eastern rim the next morning. Knowing that sooner or later someone might be picking up the trail they were leaving, he ordered the half-breed to keep a sharp eye on their back trail. For the first couple hours the cattle plodded docilely along, grabbing a mouthful of grass once in a while without stopping. The old bull was still leading the way and it was his head that came up first, smelling water. Picking up the pace, the herd was making good time when the leaders dropped down to drink from the clear water of a wide shallow creek meandering through the bottom of a shallow ravine.

'Keep that old bull a-moving,' Stokey called over to Wilson. 'Throw a rope around those horns and pull him on up the other side,' he ordered, 'otherwise the critters coming behind will bunch up and we'll be here all day.'

With the two men working together at the head, and the other gang members pushing from the rear, they got the herd watered and moving again. Throughout the day they pressed on, not hurrying the beeves too much but keeping them headed toward the bluff dead ahead.

Dropping back late in the afternoon, Stokey rode for a time alongside Curry.

'There's no reason to halt them tonight. I figure there's enough moonlight we can push them on up to the first meadow. I'll go back and help Charlie and that fool Earle kid to get them moving a little faster. You and Wilson keep the leaders bunched up and headed right.'

Not waiting for a response, the outlaw boss turned toward the rear of the herd.

★ ★ ★

Garrett had kept to one side all day, coming close enough to the herd every so often to make sure not to lose them. A couple times, staying out of sight, he'd watched, hoping to get a shot. Each time it would have been easy to knock Stokey out of the saddle and he had to hold himself back from pulling the trigger. Picking up the man's body wouldn't be so easy, though. The dead or alive reward wouldn't be his without the body.

He had noticed the big rock-faced bluff earlier in the morning and wondered if that was where they were heading. Sometime after midday he rode on ahead to take a look. Coming up to the same place Tom had ridden to earlier, he stopped. Finding the trail left behind by the earlier small jag of livestock, he could only smile.

'Now, look there, will you,' he said out loud. 'So the bad asses have a back door. And I wonder how far that trail goes up. Guess it's worth a look-see before dark. Just might be a good place up there for me to lay up.'

Keeping to one side so any marks left by his horse would be less likely to be seen, he rode up the trail.

* * *

Tom reached the bluff trail not long after the herd had passed that way. In the fading sunlight he was just able to make out the steam rising from the piles of droppings left behind. Touching a spur to the horse's flank, he slowly followed behind, not wanting to run headlong into the tail end of things.

He didn't know what to expect and stopped at a point where he could see some distance ahead. Blending into the trees at one side of the track, he studied the open field ahead and a little below where he sat. It was nothing more than a huge pasture and the first thing he spotted was the herd, a dark mass spread out some distance away. The bright twinkle of a fire indicated where the rustlers had set up camp over on the far side. In the growing darkness, it was impossible to tell how far away they were.

Thinking about it, he decided it wouldn't be wise to ride on in the night. If he was up early enough, he thought, maybe he could catch them off guard. Reining his horse off deeper into the trees he looked for a place to make camp. It was hard to be sure in the darkness of the forest, but he wound among the trees until he figured he was far enough off the trail to be safe. After hobbling his horse he dug a pit to hide his fire in.

Wanting to get moving early, he slept in short snatches. Tired from the long hours he'd spent in the saddle over the last few days, Tom knew if he let himself go, he'd likely not wake up until the sun was bright in the morning sky. Sitting with his back to a tree trunk, his body wrapped in his bedroll against the night-time coolness, he dozed, coming awake every so often.

The sound of a gunshot brought him out of the bedding just as things were starting to get light. Standing with his Colt in hand, wide awake and ready for anything, Tom hesitated. It had to have come from the raiders' camp he decided and he ran back through the trees, to stand looking out over the field.

The sun still had a few minutes before coming up but the morning air was warming. As far as he could see, the ground was covered by a thin mist, rising like cool smoke from the moist grass. Far in the distance he could just make out a few head of cattle standing on their feet, their heads turned to where a thin spiral of smoke curled upward in a gray stream. The rustlers were up and about. He'd overslept.

Running back to his camp, he quickly rolled his bedding and threw the leather onto his horse. He had noticed that the animal liked to play games in the morning, expanding its chest when someone was tightening the cinches.

'I don't have time for such foolishness,' Tom snarled, ramming his knee hard into the animal's stomach and pulling the leather bands tight. Slipping the bit in place, he swung into the saddle. There had been no more gunshots.

Keeping close to the edge of the trees, he rode at a fast walk along the edge of the field, his body tense, leaning low over the horse's neck.

19

'C'mon, you bums,' Stokey snarled.

He hadn't slept much, tossing around in his blankets. For some reason he was tense, unable to relax. This, he had decided at some point, would be the last raid he made for that damn banker. Maybe it was time to ride on, look for some new territory. Unable to sleep and still feeling edgy, when he saw the darkness starting to gray out he was ready to get going. Snarling his order, he kicked first one bedroll and then the next.

Half-breed Charlie, true to his Indian nature, came awake at the boss's first grumbling. Knowing the man's habit, he waited to be kicked out of his blankets. Maybe this time, he swore silently, maybe this time I'll not take having him kick at me.

Slipping his revolver from the holster,

he waited. This time Stokey didn't get to his side of the fire.

*　*　*

Garrett had watched as the herd came up the grade and was pushed across the grassland. All day the animals had been hurried, but now the pressure put on them from the riders bringing up the rear lessened. No longer pressed on, the cattle took up the pattern of such animals, chomping at a mouthful before taking a slow step or two only to reach down to tear at the sun-baked grass. By the time full night had come to the upper meadow, the herd had spread out, getting comfortable in their new surroundings. The flickering campfire drew the individual cows to that side of the meadow until by midnight nearly all the herd were some distance away, calmly lying in a mass, chewing their cuds.

The manhunter was certain; this was as far as he needed to go. Leaving his horse tied some distance away, he had quietly made his way through the trees until he could look down on where the gang of rustlers were eating a meal of beans and bread. Picking out the sheepskin vest of the man he'd determined was Stokey, he had slowly brought his rifle up and using a sturdy pine tree to lean against had taken careful aim. After a long minute, he had let the rifle back down. The shot was too unsure in the flickering of the campfire. He'd have to wait for better light.

Settling down with his back to the pine, he had watched the men until they turned in. Smiling a little, he had closed his eyes. Close enough to hear what the men were saying; he knew he'd be awake at the first sounds of the men getting ready for the next day's work.

It was Stokey's grumbling that had brought Garrett's head up in the morning. Blinking his eyes wide, he stood up to stand again by the tree, his rifle steady. In the camp, the round-shouldered man was going around the camp, kicking at the humped piles of blankets.

'Come on, dammit,' he heard the outlaw leader's voice snap, 'get your asses outa them blankets and let's get this show on the road.'

Garrett waited and touched the trigger when the rustler turned fully around, unknowingly facing the unseen rifleman. The man he'd identified as Stokey dropped like a stone, dead before he hit the ground.

'Don't go moving around, boys,' Garrett yelled out, letting them hear the sound of him levering another round into the chamber. 'Let's not get in the way of this, you hear?'

'Don't go shooting, mister,' someone called out after a minute. 'We ain't gonna move any.'

'What'd you want?' another called. 'We ain't got no money or nothing.'

'I don't want anything you got so just lie there quietly for a bit.'

'OK, man, we ain't moving.'

Garrett moved closer until, staying at the edge of the forest, he could see the four of them clearly.

'Now boys, here's the deal,' he said, pointing the barrel of his rifle first at one and then the other. 'I don't want any of you. I'm here for one thing. Stokey. So, what say one of you comes up slowly and easily out of that bedroll and saddles up four horses. When you're all ready to ride, you can take off. But remember, I know what you all look like. Don't go riding back over toward Ophir or anyway close to the mining district or I'll think you're after me and I'll shoot you down on sight, you understand me?'

'Yeah, man. We can go but we gotta stay away from the mining town.'

'Now, you there, you with the braids hanging down your back like Geronimo. Leave that gun belt on your blankets and go saddle up four of them horses. Shuck the rifles from those saddle scabbards, too.'

Moving slowly, Charlie slapped saddles on the horses and brought them close to the unlit morning fire.

'All right, one at a time, climb aboard and head out. You won't need your weapons so leave them behind.'

'Man,' the outlaw with screwy eyes complained, 'you can't send us out without our guns. Hell, we ain't even had coffee yet.'

Garrett held his rifle tight on the man. He thought he was hidden from their view by some brush but he wasn't sure. Anyway, he couldn't tell whether this man was looking his way or not.

'Don't worry about it. You won't starve. Oh, and with all the rustling you've done, I wouldn't be so quick to head back down into the basin, either. There's a lot of angry ranchers down there.'

'That means we got to go on up over the pass,' one of them said, shaking his head. Garrett had never learned his name. 'That's mighty close to the mining district.'

'Just don't stop. I'll be coming somewhere behind and I'd better not catch up with any of you. Don't go taking your time. OK,' Garrett called after giving them a minute to think about his words. 'That's enough talk. You there, Jesse Earle. I knew your brothers, Rufus and Harlan, bastards both and so probably are you. But that's the way of it. Anyhow, I can put a name to you and that's enough, you take out first. Just don't let me see you in these parts again.'

'Go to hell, whoever you are,' the youngster muttered reaching for the reins of the nearest horse. Swinging aboard, he jerked the horse's head around and rode out. Garrett didn't take his eyes off the others and didn't see which way Earle went.

20

'Damn him!' Earle fumed as he cruelly jabbed both spurs into the animal. 'Calling me a bastard like that.' Then remembering how easily the man had killed Stokey, he sobered. 'Hells bells, he coulda done us all in.'

Pulling back on the reins he sat still letting his anger fade. It wouldn't do any good to just go barreling up over the pass like that damn fool that killed the boss ordered so he'd angled off to one side. Sitting there trying to think what to do and where to go, he frowned in thought. The only place he was halfway familiar with was Ophir but they'd all been warned away from that, hadn't they? For the first time he faced life without his older brothers to tell him what to do. He didn't want to think about his two brothers.

'I wonder why that feller with the

rifle didn't shoot us all,' he muttered, sitting relaxed in the saddle. 'Guess Stokey was the only one people knew about. Yeah, that idiot Curry, he certainly wanted everyone to know how tough he was, but, shucks, he wasn't so very much. Nope, it had to be that old Hank had some money on his head. Serves him right,' Earle snorted, causing his horse to take a sudden step.

'Whoa up there, you piece of crow bait,' Earle ordered, jerking back on the leather reins.

The horse had been the closest one and when told to ride he hadn't wanted to waste any time. He'd grabbed the first that came to hand. Looking the animal over he seemed to remember seeing that half-breed, Charlie, riding it. Well, it was his now. At least until he could steal a better one.

Reaching back, he pulled the worn and patched saddle-bags free and started going through them. He grimaced when his hand touched something that felt slimy. Using two fingers he drew what looked to be the skin from some kind of animal from one of the bags.

'Gawd, I'll bet old Charlie carried this thing wanting to make everyone believe it was a scalp. Looks more like a piece cut off the back of some kind of dog or something. Ugh,' he made a face and threw it away. A shirt, smelling musty and, Earle thought, likely to be filled with a crowd of chiggers and other crawly critters was about all that remained in that side. Unbuckling the other bag he hit paydirt, a short-barreled revolver.

'Now, how about that,' the youngster smiled coldly. 'Ain't as good as that .44 I had to leave behind, but it's a helluva lot better than nothing.'

Quickly checking the cylinder, he found all chambers filled.

'A .38. Damn, I'll have to be right on top of anyone to do any real damage,' he said disapprovingly.

The pistol was too small for his holster so he simply shoved it under the belt that held up his pants.

All right, he asked silently, what now?

For the first time he really missed his brothers. Not that they'd ever done anything to make his life better or taught him anything except how to steal. And as far back as he could remember, they'd taught him by yelling or kicking him. But they were his only kinfolk. That made all the difference, as far as he could see. Why, he couldn't leave the Ferris Corners area without doing something about that slick what'd killed both Rufus and Harlan. OK, so he wasn't part of any gang anymore. Well, he'd never really been accepted by old Hank, had he? Nope. It served the outlaw right, getting hisself killed like that.

He figured the others had been chased out of the camp and sent on their way. They must have done what they'd been told and headed for the high country and the pass. Well, that wasn't for him. He was going the other way, back to Ferris Corners. Maybe that banker feller would have some work for him.

Nodding and feeling better for having made a decision, he neck-reined the horse around and set out at a trot, keeping to the edge of the trees so that the rifleman wouldn't see him in the coming daylight.

21

Victor Garrett felt good, real good. Five thousand dollars. There was a lot he could do with five thousand dollars. That was how much he had tied to the back of that sorrel gelding, the only horse left behind when the Indian rustler and his cockeyed partner rode off.

He'd made the Indian go first and held the other man back for a few minutes. Likely the two would join up somewhere up the trail, possibly even with the first one, young Earle. There was nothing he could do about that and it didn't really matter. As far as he could see, after shooting Stokey he only had two options, kill all the others or let them ride out. Even knowing they could if they wanted, team up and shoot him, he couldn't shoot all three of them. Shooting the outlaw in the back didn't bother him; Stokey was worth real money and the others weren't. Anyway, shooting those fools in cold blood was not his style. Sometimes he didn't understand himself.

The sorrel didn't like having the body tied across the saddle and had reared when Garrett had first attempted to drape it over the leather. He'd had to tie the horse's head tight against a tree trunk to get it to hold still long enough to get the job done. Wrapping Stokey in a blanket had helped. At least it appeared to; when Garrett removed the bridle leaving a lead rope tied around the sorrel's neck the horse settled down and even started chomping at some grass.

With the body secure and the sorrel's lead tied to a tree he strode back to where he'd left his horse tied and rode back into the camp. Tying both animals on enough lead that they could reach grass, Garrett went back to the campfire.

'Well, now,' the manhunter mumbled

to himself. Kicking a couple sticks onto the coals he picked up the fire-scorched coffee pot and sloshed it around. 'Might as well not waste this,' he went on talking to himself.

Hunkered down to balance the pot on a pair of flat rocks he froze at the sound of a single gun shot. Quickly leaving the pot next to the little blaze, and without standing up, he duck-walked away, staying low until he was in the protection of the trees. Listening he tried to figure what the gunshot could mean. Waiting for whatever was to happen, he looked over to where the horses stood. His rifle was over there in the saddle scabbard. All he had was his six-shot Colt. Glancing over at the weapons left lying on the three bedrolls he waited, wishing he could reach them.

He slowly rose to stand next to a pine for what seemed a long time, his eyes scanning the field beyond the camp, listening. The horses, the sorrel having forgotten all about the man tied over its back, moved from one clump of grass to another, grazing. A few head of beef — all he could see of the small herd — were doing the same. The only sounds he could hear were the morning breeze blowing through the tops of the trees and the bubbling of the coffee boiling.

'Damn,' the hidden man snorted and then, deciding the gunfire had nothing to do with him, he dashed over to move the pot away from the fire, burning his fingers.

Cursing he jerked his hand away, nearly tipping the pot over. 'Damn!' he snarled, then remembering how out in the open he was, ducked down to look around quickly. None of the animals was paying any attention. Slowly, he relaxed and, picking up a tin cup that had been left behind, he poured what was left in the pot. There wasn't much and it was blacker than the inside of a hole in the ground at midnight. If he took the time for the cup of coffee, he figured, it would give the three bad men the chance to get far enough ahead so he wouldn't likely run into them.

Sipping at the hot brew, Garrett thought about the single gun shot. 'I wonder who was doing the shooting,' he mused aloud. 'I made those damn fools leave their firearms when they rode out, so it couldn't have been any of them. Not likely anyone else would be riding around up here.' He'd have to be watchful when he rode out.

Simply dropping the cup when he was finished, he kicked the rocks and some dirt over what was left of the fire. Sitting on the back of his horse and holding the lead rope tied to the sorrel, he looked out at the grazing cattle.

'Guess someone'll come along and find these,' he said, nodding. 'Ain't nothing for me here. I got what I came for. C'mon, horse, let's get outa here.'

Feeling pretty good, he gigged his mount, turning back into the trees and heading up and away from the field.

Slowly as the warmth of the morning sun eased the stiffness of his back muscles, he relaxed. For the first time since following that fool Earle out of Ferris Corners, he felt his body unwind. Getting to Ophir and getting rid of this body was next and it couldn't happen soon enough. That same warmth he was feeling on his back would be making things difficult for Stokey.

When he got to the place on the trail where one of the horsemen had turned off, he hesitated. The morning sun made the sign clear; one of those three renegades hadn't done what he'd told them. Sitting there thinking about it, and remembering the gunshot he'd heard, he wondered.

'Now what would make one of them circle around?' he asked, studying the tracks left in the soft soil. 'Not to come back after me,' he went on. 'None of them would have any reason for that. Could be this jasper had thoughts about that herd?' Shaking his head and pursing his lips he frowned. That didn't seem likely either.

Curiosity got the best of him. 'Now I

certainly wouldn't want someone on my back trail. C'mon, horse, let's take a look and see what this feller was up to.' Reining around and easing his rifle in the scabbard, he set out to follow the unknown horseman.

Riding slowly, he studied the tracks. Whoever it was, the rider had stopped at one point for some reason. The horse had stood for a time then minced about a little, probably bored. That could mean the rider was waiting or maybe sitting and thinking about what to do next. Whatever the reason, the horse then left that place and continued on. Still there was no indication who it was or where he was going. The trail, though, was now more in a steady direction. Garrett read the sign and figured the rider was heading around the grass-covered field and was heading back to town.

With that thought, he stopped his horse. No reason to go on following the rider. It didn't matter who it'd been. Let him go, Garrett decided and was turning back when he heard someone groan. Panicked, he grabbed his rifle and slid out of the saddle.

Keeping the rifle ready, he dropped the reins, ground-hitching his horse. Crouching low he started moving through the trees toward where he thought the sound had come from. Freezing when he heard another soft moan, he waited. Deciding what he'd heard wasn't the sound someone would make if setting up an ambush, the manhunter went forward, taking advantage of the trees around him for cover.

Keeping his eyes searching the forest he almost stepped on the man's body when he circled around one huge pine tree.

'What the — ?' he snarled, jumping back and bringing his rifle down to aim at the man's back. 'Don't move, stranger. You're covered from here to breakfast.'

A worn, dirty gray Stetson half-hid the man's head. The head didn't move and Garrett got no answer.

Kneeling Garrett cautiously felt the back of the man's neck. A strong pulse beat against his fingers. The man didn't move at the touch. Moving slowly and carefully, he leaned his rifle against the tree trunk and holding his Colt with one hand reached out to lift the hat. Drying blood, still shiny in spots but starting to take on a dull blackness, caked the side of the man's head.

'So that's what the shooting was all about. Mister, someone surely didn't like you.'

Turning the wounded man gently over, he sat back nodding, having recognized the cowboy.

'Tom Bantry. And I'll wager I know which of those bad asses it was that done this,' he said quietly. 'Young Earle was the only one I know of that would have seen you in town. Now why would he shoot you, I wonder. And where did he get the gun?'

Glancing down he saw that the cowboy's holster was empty. Earle had taken the man's handgun. Close by the wounded man's leg, half-hidden in the pine needles, he spotted a smaller revolver.

Picking it up, he sniffed at the barrel.

'Uh-huh. Somebody lost his shooter, a .38. Now if Earle had used a .44 you'd be one dead man, Bantry. This little peashooter didn't do more that break the skin and give you a headache, I'll wager. Well, ain't you the lucky one.'

Glancing back over his shoulder and thinking about Stokey's body tied on the back of that horse, he cursed, 'Ah, hell. I can't just leave you here, now can I?'

Leaning down to give the head wound a closer inspection, he nodded. 'Yes, I can. Old Hank back there won't last long in the day's heat and that five thousand dollars is more important to me. Sorry, old man,' he said having made his decision and standing up.

22

He had just picked up his rifle when the man on the ground let out a long sigh.

'Water,' the wounded man muttered, not opening his eyes. 'You happen to have a bit of water?' Bantry said weakly.

Garrett frowned, cursing silently. 'Well, hell, so you're not so close to dead as you thought. Yeah, wait a minute and I'll get my canteen.'

After letting the cowboy drink, he used some of the water and his neckerchief to mop at the gash on Bantry's head.

'Now that wound don't look all that bad,' he said, finishing up by wrapping the damp cloth around Bantry's skull. 'It's likely you woke up with a headache but, well, dammit, it don't look so bad as to kill you.'

'Hmmm,' Bantry moaned softly. 'I can hear you all right, but my eyes don't seem to want to focus, everything's blurry. And yes, there are a couple drums beating in my head.'

'That's likely, getting shot like that can do that. From what I see, it looks like the bullet only cut the skin, bouncing off your skull bone. A blow like that can do funny things to a man's brainpan. My name's Garrett by the way, Victor Garrett.'

'Tom Bantry. Glad to make your acquaintance. Is there any more water in that canteen?'

'Who shot you and why?' Garrett asked, settling back on his heels.

'I didn't see who it was. Some rider came barreling out of the trees, caught me totally unprepared, damn fool that I was. I'd been riding along trying to be quiet and he came out of the trees shooting. Next thing I know I'm on my back in the dirt, sometimes awake and sometimes not. Then I heard you muttering to yourself. What did you say your name was?'

'Victor Garrett. I'm from over Ophir

way. So, someone riding fast through the trees. I got to figure it was young Earle what did it to you. A sorry piece of work he is, too. It'd be something he'd do. But what the hell you doing riding out here, if I might ask?'

'Hunting after a bunch of cattle. I was following behind some rustlers who'd taken a small herd from a ranch back down in the basin. You didn't come across them, by any chance,' he asked, his words coming slow as he started to lose consciousness.

'Yeah,' Garrett started to tell him but stopped when he saw that Bantry was down for the count. 'Damn it all to hell, don't go to sleep on me. I got places to go and things to do.'

For a time he just sat, watching Bantry lie on the forest floor unmoving. Well, he could climb back into the saddle and ride on up over the pass to Ophir. Get rid of old Hard Luck Hank before he started to stink, take his money and then what? His plans only took him so far.

So maybe this wasn't a good time to burn bridges. It couldn't hurt him much to help this feller out. After all, having a rancher or a rancher's son in his debt might come in handy somewhere down the line. Hearing a horse blow somewhere farther back in the brush decided it for him. Wandering back, Garrett caught up the reins and walked back to where Bantry lay.

With the wounded man tied to his own saddle, Garrett rode back to where Stokey had set up camp, towing both horses behind him. Leaving two of the horses out in the grass, tying the sorrel in the shadow of a tree, he set Bantry on a pile of blankets left behind by the rustlers. Garrett was wondering what to do when the young man's eyes came open.

'Oh, God,' Bantry moaned, turning to one side holding both hands to his head.

'Welcome back,' Garrett said softly. 'Head still pounding, I take it. Well, I reckon you can count on that for a few

228

more days. How're the eyes, things still blurry?'

Moving slowly, Tom Bantry moved one hand and let his eyelids inch up. 'Yeah,' he answered, his words almost a whisper. 'Things are a blur and my head feels like it's going to explode.'

Garrett looked around, thinking of what he could do.

'Look, Bantry, I can't do anything about that. And,' glancing over at the sorrel with its blanket wrapped load, he grimaced, 'I can't spend much time hanging around here. Nothing I can do anyhow. Listen, there's enough food here, left behind by those rustlers you were chasing. They've ridden out and won't be back. Earle was one of them but I don't think he'll be coming back this way either. Likely gone on into town. There's a spring over there a piece, so you got water. I'll hobble your horse and hang the saddle so you can find it when you're feeling better. I'd figure if you lay back and sleep as much as you can, let nature take its course, you'll be better in a couple days.'

Bantry didn't move.

'Tell you what,' Garrett went on, 'I'll heat up a pot of coffee for you, then I got to be riding. I hate to leave you like this, but there ain't nothing more I can do.'

'Did I hear you say you thought it was Earle that shot me?' Bantry said, still not moving.

'Yeah, it figures. Far as I know he'd be the only one out there about then. I heard the shot but had other things to take care of. It's hard to say why he'd be so ready to shoot you down. Probably scared the hell out of him, coming on to you like that and he just reacted.'

'Maybe. But he might have been hunting me. I shot both his brothers, you know.'

That news stopped Garrett. 'Yeah, I was there in the saloon when Harlan Earle got his. I didn't know you'd done in Rufus, too.'

'He came at me with a shotgun. For

some reason he had a young girl, a woman really, tied to a bunk in his cabin. I never did figure that out. Looked like he was keeping the girl and her brother prisoner. I don't know.'

Putting the filled pot on the flat rocks next to the fire, Garrett looked over at the man. 'A young girl and her brother you say? Did they mention their name?

'Uh-huh. Carlyle. Cora Lee and Bobby Carlyle.'

'Whew, so that's what happened to them.'

'What do you mean,' Tom Bantry's voice was getting weaker but he was fighting to stay awake.

'It was over in Ophir, the last time anyone saw Carlyle's kids. Edgar Carlyle was one of the early miners, had a share in one of the mines. Was doing real good, had been part of Ophir's mining community from the earlier days. There was Edgar and his wife and the two kids. Then the missus died, took on some kind of sickness and just died. That hit old Edgar pretty hard. He took to drinking and wasn't long before he'd lost everything, the mine, their house, everything.'

'What happened to the two kids?'

'Well, I'm not sure. The story is that Edgar lost them in a poker game. Lost them and his last horses, a wagon and the kids to Rufus Earle. You gotta understand. Rufus Earle wasn't much liked in the mining district, but nobody could catch him at anything. It wasn't that he was smarter'n anyone. Actually most thought he was missing a few cards from having a full deck. He was just damn lucky, I always figured. Anyway, it was said he had a liking for young girls. Rumor had it that he almost got hung out in California for messing with a young girl. Turned out to be the daughter of someone important in whatever mining camp they were in. What we heard was that his older brother, Harlan shot up the town and got him out of jail the morning Rufus was to hang. Anyway, they both turned up over in Ophir. But

I heard that when Edgar woke up to discover he'd gone and gambled away his kids he shot himself dead.'

Neither man spoke. The only sound for a while was the bubbling of the boiling water. Garrett sat still, staring into the fire while remembering. Shaking himself as if coming awake, he glanced over at Bantry.

The wounded man's hands had relaxed, falling away from his head. Getting close, he saw how the young man was lying all relaxed, fast asleep. The wound hadn't bled anymore.

'Well, partner, that's it,' he said quietly. 'I'll leave you the coffee but there ain't nothing else I can do. You take it easy for a few days and you'll either be dead or all right.'

Doing what he said he'd do, Garrett hobbled Bantry's horse before taking up the sorrel's lead rope and with a last look around, rode out of the camp.

23

He'd done it; he'd killed that rancher who had shot both his brothers. Jesse Earle rode on, a big satisfied smile on his face. Now let anyone tell him to his face that he was just a punk kid. Once the story got around everyone would know that when you dealt wrong with Jesse Earle you were dealing with trouble.

Reliving the shooting, he felt like giggling. Oh, the look on that feller's face when he came out from behind that tree to see nothing but the barrel of that little pistol staring at him. Bang — Earle snorted happily at the memory — one to the head and he was dead. Serves him right, after what he'd done to Rufus and Harlan.

This time Jesse Earle did giggle.

'Wal, hoss, there ain't no reason to be riding up here in the trees. Won't nobody be coming along behind us. Let's get down in the grass and be comfortable.'

Keeping the horse to an easy trot, Jesse Earle sat as tall in the saddle as he could, his shoulders back and head held high. The morning might have started out bad but didn't things turn out right? Riding easy he crossed the end of the grassy pocket just as the sun was coming up, thinking about all that had happened. Won't that banker down in town be nearly as happy, knowing what has happened, he silently asked himself.

Nodding, he smiled at his luck. Likely there wouldn't have been much money coming from that little bitty herd anyway but maybe that banker Sidwell'd give him some riding money when he heard that the owner of them animals was lying up there in the trees. It'd be quite a while before anybody came looking for them cows and that seemed to be what the banker wanted.

Thinking back, he hadn't liked getting kicked out of their camp but what could he do? It wasn't fair, he frowned at the thought, having that backshooter, whoever he was, not giving Stokey or any of them a chance, shooting out of the trees like that. Thinking about it now though, he decided it was all for the better. If'n they'd been left alone, that man, Bantry, woulda come riding in when they was just starting to move the herd toward the pass. Yeah. Maybe it all worked out pretty good anyhow.

Remembering about the way it all happened, he thought it was kinda funny. First with Stokey getting hisself shot like that meant there wouldn't be any more rustling or going back to raid the gold miners. Well, maybe it wouldn't matter none. When people learned about what he'd done, he wouldn't have any trouble getting in with another gang. This time, he swore silently, it'd be with someone who knew how to do things. Rustling a few head here and there wasn't bringing in any real money. No sir, the smart money was in the banks. Like that one old Sidwell ran. Now, there was something to think about.

First, though, he'd have to let everyone know what'd happened. Earle's thin smile returned as he saw himself standing at the bar there in Ferris Corners telling everyone about the shooting.

'Yeah, it was a complete surprise, that feller what killed my brothers came out of the trees, his six-gun ablaze. Well, what could I do? All I had was time to defend myself. His shots all missed and mine didn't.'

Oh, yeah, he'd have them all listening, that's for sure.

* * *

Tom Bantry wasn't awake when Garrett rode out. The next time he tried to open his eyes, it was late afternoon and the warmth from the sun had gone as the deep shadows started blanketing the little valley. Still half-asleep and feeling a chill, the wounded man reached out for a blanket. The movement brought back the throbbing behind his eyes. Groaning, he fell back.

Not moving, he let the curtain of pain settle a bit, his thinking not making any sense. As the hurting drew back, images came out of the gray cotton that seemed to fill his head. Vaguely he recalled hearing someone, a man, telling him something about resting. Trying to make sense of it, he drifted once again into sleep.

Later, the hacking of his dry throat jerked him awake. The movement jolted his head, sending a knife-sharp stab of agony across the top of his skull. For a few long minutes he lay still, willing the pain to leave him alone. A fit of dry coughing forced him to sit up. Opening his eyes to blackness, fear that he'd gone blind enveloped him. Slowly as his eyes adjusted, he began to make out the distorted outline of trees against the starlit sky. The pinpoints of light themselves looked to be somewhere on the other side of a gray fog.

Blurry, he remembered; back in day light everything had been blurry and out of focus. Now, by closing one eye, even in the darkness of the night, he was able to make out his surroundings. Close to hand, he saw in the faint glow from a dying bed of coals, was a tin coffee pot. Most of the liquid had boiled away, but enough remained to wet his throat.

Drinking straight from the pot, he let the strong liquid seep down his throat. Moving slowly, he wrapped one of the blankets he'd been lying on around his shoulders and sat back. Keeping his right eye closed helped his vision. With both eyes open everything was hazy and unclear. Experimenting a little, he found that the trouble was with his right eye. Closing that eye he let his gaze take in things. Nothing was familiar.

The last he could remember was the surprise when a rider came barreling out of the trees in front of him, his horse rearing back and then a clout against his head.

Then there was the memory of someone, a man, telling him to sleep, the words seeming to echo in his mind. Not sure of that, he felt his open eye droop and after taking another drink of coffee, crawled back into the blankets.

It was morning when he next opened his eyes. Lying unmoving, he watched as a big, fluffy cloud moved across the sky above the tops of a half-dozen pine trees. The treetops were moving gently back and forth, pushed by a soft breeze. They were indistinct until he closed his right eye. Keeping that eyelid down, he sat up and looked around.

The bed of coals of the campfire, with its surround of fire-blackened flat stones, was near his right hand. A coffee pot, as black as the rocks, lay on its side in the dirt. Listening he caught the sound of cows mixed with the soft breeze blowing through the upper tree limbs. The cows were some distance away.

Water was the first thing; his throat felt like it was filled with dry creek sand.

Water from a spring and hard day-old dry biscuits he found in a grub sack was his breakfast. Eating slowly he remembered.

'A new day,' he said out loud between mouthfuls of the dry, crumbling bread, 'and I'm still alive.'

Carefully removing the dirty white handkerchief from around his head, he put a hand to the source of the ache and touched the tender spot on his head with gentle fingers. Rubbing it gently, he felt a hard, crusty scab covering the wound left by the bullet.

Vaguely at first, he started remembering what had happened. He'd been riding through the trees, circling around the little pocket of grass and the small herd he'd been following. At first light, after waiting through the night, he had intended to get as close to the rustlers as he could when someone had shot him.

One of the Earle boys, someone had told him. That man, Bantry shook his head in frustration at not being able to remember his name, then it came to him, Victor Garrett. A man calling himself Victor Garrett from over to Ophir. Yeah. He had said something about the Earles. Whatever that story had been was gone. The next thing was waking up this morning. Seeing the bedrolls lying around the fire pit, Bantry figured he was in the rustlers' camp. With that thought, and still keeping one eye closed, he felt for his Colt finding a little shiny, silvered revolver deep in the holster.

'Wonder where this came from?' he asked shaking his head a little side to side.

Most of the day he stayed on the blankets, next to the camp fire, which he slowly fed small sticks that the rustlers had left behind. Keeping the coffee pot warm gave him some-thing to do, that and dozing took up the entire day.

The next day, with the throbbing in his head easing, he walked out to look over the little meadow. Keeping his one eye closed still helped; things only got blurry when both were open. The blurriness didn't seem to be as bad as before. The cattle had scattered but from what he could see, they were all there. His pony, still hobbled, seemed comfortable in the tall grass and didn't pay the man any attention.

Rest, he recalled Garrett telling him, would take care of things. That appeared to be working, today there was less pain than the day before, and his vision was a little better. The only problem was that the grub sack left behind was about empty. Whether he was ready or not, he was going to have to head back down to the basin.

Lying with his back against a tree trunk that night, staring into the dying fire with his eyes open, he mentally counted the days. As far as he could make it, he had two maybe three days until the bank loan came due. It would take a little more than a day to get back to the ranch, another day to get a crew up here and then a couple days to move the herd down to the shipping pens. Figure just over a week.

Mentally picturing the countryside, he thought he could make it into town a little quicker than to the ranch. So, he decided, the thing to do would be to ride into town, getting there a day or so before the loan was delinquent and have Silas extend the loan by, say, ten days. Going directly into town, he'd have old Doc Lewis take a look at his head.

Sipping the last of the lukewarm coffee, he rolled into the blankets and fell into a sound sleep.

24

As usual, Silas Sidwell wasn't happy about seeing Jesse Earle, throwing the pen he'd been using across the room in disgust when the young man came through the back door.

'Now what the hell is it?' Sidwell snarled. 'The only time you come into town is to bring bad news. And how many times do I have to tell you not to come in here. You're supposed to be out there somewhere, keeping an eye on the work I send your way.'

Earle, still feeling proud of himself, leaned a shoulder against the closed door, folding his arms across his bony chest and letting one side of his mouth lift in a smile. He'd been thinking about this meeting ever since saddling up this morning. It hadn't been a good night for him, not having anything for supper and then only having the saddle blanket to wrap up in. Up long before even the first signs of the false dawn, he figured he made five or six miles before the sun came over the far mountain range. Until then he rode shivering in the saddle. Not having food or coffee made him decide whatever this fool of a banker would offer him wasn't going to be enough.

'I just thought you'd like to know a few things that've been happening,' Earle said calmly. He'd given it a lot of thought on the ride in, what he'd be telling the banker and how he'd say it. Especially how he'd say the words, exactly what would sound the best. The banker had to know right off that this wasn't the same messenger boy he'd been used to. No sir. Jesse Earle was now someone people would listen to, respect even. At least they would once they heard how he'd avenged his brothers.

Thinking all this out, he'd even practiced what he'd say. How he'd sound was important, he figured. Make the banker understand that things had changed.

Sidwell sat for a moment waiting for the rest of whatever the young fool had to say. 'Well,' he said eventually, 'spit it out. What has been happening that's so important you're here instead of out with that herd?'

'That herd is up in a little pocket of grass all ready to be pushed over the pass. But that's not the most important thing.' There, stretch it out a little. That'll make this self-important dude sit up and pay attention. As far as he could tell, his words were coming out strong, serious even.

The banker, again waiting to hear what this was all about, thought the young fool was sounding scared. Damn it, he thought, that herd had better be long gone. 'So, if that's the case then why in hell are you here?'

Earle nodded. 'It's that cowboy, the son of the man what owns that herd, Bantry? He's dead.'

Earle was proud of the way he said it,

sounding sure of himself, sure of his facts. He expected Sidwell to smile, maybe even motion for him to sit in one of the wooden chairs in front of the desk. It didn't happen.

'What do you mean, Bantry's dead?'

'Why, just that. Maybe you didn't know it but he killed both my brothers. Shot both Rufus and Harlan, he did. Well,' Earle slowed down and let another smile shape his words, 'I paid him back. Shot him outa the saddle. He's a dead 'un. That's for sure.'

The banker's reaction wasn't what he expected. 'In the first place,' Sidwell said, his tone hard, 'I don't care about your brothers. From what I heard, Rufus was a fool and Harlan no more than a bully. I do care, however, about Tom Bantry. It's important to me that he lives to see what I have planned. Now, explain what you're talking about and stop wasting my time.'

This wasn't the way Earle thought it'd be. No longer sure of himself, he hesitated.

'C'mon, dammit,' Sidwell snapped, 'spit it out. Did Stokey get the herd off the Flying B range or not?'

'Yeah, I said that. We ran them up into a little valley, up off the floor of the basin. That's when some jasper came into our camp and shot the boss.'

'What? What the hell are you talking about, shot the boss. First you say you shot Tom and now you're claiming someone shot Stokey?'

'Well, yeah, that's what happened. It was coming on sunup a couple days ago and we was just getting outa our blankets when someone backshot him. Drilled him clean. Stokey. Then the man made us saddle up and ride out. Warned us not to let him ever see us again and . . . ' Earle let the words fade out. He could see Sidwell wasn't interested in that part of it.

'First off, who was this man you say backshot Stokey?'

'Hell, I don't know. None of us had ever seen him before. He just stayed back in the brush a little, you know, and made us ride out. One at a time, like. Old Curry and Charlie, I expect they rode on over the pass. I dunno about them. I wanted to get that Bantry feller for killing my kin so I came back this way.'

'And ambushed Tom Bantry,' Sidwell finished the story. Earle could only nod. Somehow none of this seemed to have any significance for the banker.

'I figured you'd want to know so I came back here as fast as I could.'

Sidwell walked around to pick up the pen he'd thrown down and, deep in thought, went back to sit at his desk, idly dipping the nib in and out of the ink well. Earle didn't know what to do so he just stood still, not saying another word.

'The cattle are up in the foothills, you say? Too far to be brought back down before the end of the week?'

'Oh, yeah, it'd take at least that long,' Earle said hurriedly, 'if'n someone was to start pushing them today. And ain't nobody knows they're up there. That little jag ain't going nowhere for a while.'

'And Stokey's dead and the rest of his gang has been chased out of the country, is that what you're telling me?'

'Uh-huh, that's right, Mister Sidwell.'

'What are you planning on doing?'

'Well, I don't rightly know. To tell the truth, I was hoping you'd have something for me. Work I mean,' he added quickly.

'Hmm,' Sidwell thought about it and then nodded. 'Yes, maybe I do.'

Opening a desk drawer he picked up a handful of coins and handed them across to the young man. 'Here, this will carry you over for a couple days. Stay away from here and stay out of the saloon. I don't want you to go drinking and telling anyone about any of this. Hear me?'

Earle quickly nodded.

'OK, day after tomorrow, soon after breakfast you come back here, no,' he hesitated then went on, 'no, better you don't come here any more. Day after tomorrow you get your horse and wait for me about a mile out of town, out toward that rocky place on the road toward the Flying B. Can you remember all that?'

'Yes, sir. Stay out of trouble, don't talk to anyone and meet you out on the road the morning after tomorrow. What're we going to do?'

'Don't worry about that. Just do what you're told. Now get out of here.' Dismissing the man, Sidwell went back to looking at the paper he'd been working on.

25

The sight in Bantry's right eye was getting better. Each time he tested it by putting a hand over the other eye the fuzziness around the edges was a little less bothersome. Give it some rest that man, Garrett, had told him and rest he'd been doing. That's all he'd been doing but he was getting twitchy. Cabin fever, he thought, even if there was no cabin. Anyway, he thought it'd be better to ride in and talk with Silas before the note came due.

The first day or so he hadn't done much more than sleep, getting out of the blankets only to get a drink of water or relieve himself. Somewhere in the late afternoon of the next day he had woken up with the feeling he'd probably never need sleep again. That was when he had dug through the belongings left behind and found the grub sack. There wasn't much in the way of food there, but he had made do with what there was. Luckily the sack of coffee beans had been full.

He hadn't moved around a great deal the rest of that day, mostly just sitting and studying the little valley that lay out before him, all the time keeping one eye closed. His headache had grown fainter and remembering it he was surprised to find it almost gone. He hadn't really noticed. Now it was only the helplessness he felt in not being able to see clearly. But even that he thought was passing.

He'd been sure he had had enough of sleeping until after eating a meal and still sitting on the bedroll he'd been using, he caught himself dozing off. Soon after the sun went down he felt his eyes closing. Putting his half-full coffee cup aside he leaned over and fell asleep.

The next morning he came awake with the sun. His right arm ached where he'd been lying on it all night.

Moving slowly, he dug around in the fire pit until he found a small handful of coals and soon had a small fire blazing. Moving his arm around as he filled the coffee pot with water and set it on a couple flat rocks, he walked out to see how things were while the coffee brewed.

Stepping out into the open, he spotted his horse, its head coming up to watch him before going back to grazing. Well, he said to himself, at least I won't have to walk back to town. His herd was spread all over the place, none of them paying either him or the horse any mind. A little breeze blowing down from higher up put movement to the tops of cat-tails growing along the banks of a small marshy pond over on the far side. Old Harvey had said there was plenty of water up here.

For the first time since being carried into the camp he took a good look at the area he found himself in. Actually no more than a grassy wide swale with the trail cutting through it, the bowl appeared to take in about twenty acres or so. Already the herd had made a noticeable mark on the feed that had been growing there. They'd have to be moved soon, he saw.

The spring near the camp was only one of many, the water from them feeding the pond and then pouring out to make a small creek that disappeared somewhere around the base of a huge sandstone boulder. The churned-up dirt alongside that boulder told him where the trail was. Most likely the flowing creek went underground there only to come out somewhere down on the flats. This, he thought, was the first of the series of small meadows that Harvey had talked about. Someday he'd have to come up and look it all over, but not now. Now he had to get himself down the trail to town.

Feeling rested, and almost being able to see out of both eyes, Bantry spent the morning checking out the weapons that had been left behind. On the piles of blankets he'd found two Henrys and a Model 87 lever action Winchester shotgun, a little pocket derringer and three Colt revolvers. These he had to believe came from the rustlers and it was obvious they liked to be well armed. All of the weapons were rust free and well oiled, although the bluing on one of the Colts and both Henry rifles had worn thin.

Bantry had never seen that kind of shotgun before. His pa used a pump action double-barreled shotgun for duck hunting. Some time or another he'd seen an article in a magazine about the lever action model but wasn't able to remember what he'd read about it. After carefully ejecting the five 12-gauge shells from the tube magazine, he took some time to look it over. After swinging the weapon up to his shoulder he decided it was a little heavier than his Henry. Looking down the barrel at the front sight all he could make out was the tiny smudge that was the front sight. He quickly closed that eye and went on to inspect the other firearms.

Remembering the little silver .38 pistol, he concluded it had been left behind by Jesse Earle, who had then taken his .44 caliber Colt. Scrutinizing the three Colts left behind, he chose one, tossing the other back onto the blankets. The cylinder on that one, he noticed, had a loose feel to it. Unloading the weapon, he examined the shells for dirt or rust before reloading. He hadn't really missed the Colt that Earle had taken but once this one was slipped into the worn leather holster he somehow felt better.

The last of the rock-hard biscuits was eaten by dunking them in a cup of coffee. He ate that meal slow, stretching it out as long as he could. Another reason to start back toward town. As it was, it'd be a long empty ride.

That evening, not feeling like sleep yet, he sat with his back against a tree looking out at the little meadow. The moon coming up over the far mountain tops gave enough light for him to be able to make out most everything. His horse, hobbled but curious, came shambling over, snorting and making whoofing sounds as it got close enough to nudge the man's leg.

'You think you're about ready to head out, hoss?' Bantry asked, not expecting to get an answer. 'Well, me too. I still can't see all that clearly, but things are getting better. Maybe by the time we get to talk with Doc Lewis I won't need his advice. Anyhow, we got to stop by the bank and talk with Silas. I figure that's first, then go out to the Flying B to see how many men we're still paying and get a few of them to come up here to gather up these critters. Yeah, and it'd be good to see how Miss Cora Lee is getting on.'

Thinking about the young woman, he remembered what Garrett had said about Rufus Earle. 'I wonder if there's anything to that story. Doesn't seem like something a father would do, gamble off his daughter. And what about Bobby? Would the boy be part of a wager? That's not something I've ever heard of anybody doing before.'

Relaxed and watching the moon and the evening stars in the far sky, he wondered about that. That feller wouldn't have a reason to make up a story like that, would he? Not with Rufus dead, he wouldn't. It couldn't hurt the man now that he was dead. But maybe it was true and the upset of it all had something to do with her not being able to talk. Strange things could happen, he nodded, agreeing with himself. Hadn't Mattie Andrews said something about Cora starting to speak? Well, who knows, maybe by now she was jabbering away like any other woman. Yes, he'd have to stop by and see how things were there.

The vision in his right eye was a lot better the next morning. Up before the sun, he saddled his horse and rode out, leaving all the rustlers' belongings behind, except for someone's Colt. After bundling up the other weapons in one of the blankets, he tied them to a tree limb as high as he could reach.

He'd pick that bundle up when coming up to get the herd.

Riding at a steady pace, alternating between a ground-eating lope and a brisk trot, and stopping every so often to let his horse blow, he made good time. Supper that night was a couple cups of coffee. His horse, after being stripped of the saddle and bridle, had rolled in the dirt and fed its fill on grass. Tom Bantry crawled into the blankets with his stomach growling.

26

Breakfast was a cup of warmed-up coffee. With hunger making its own noises, he wasted no time in riding the remaining distance into Ferris Corners. After taking time to give his horse a quick currying and a bait of oats, Bantry made for the Mexican's restaurant.

'Hey, look who's here,' Deputy Sheriff Sullivan called out as the cowboy walked in. Bantry stopped when he saw Horace Davis sitting at the table.

The horse breeder nodded his greeting. 'Heard tell you was out trying to run down that gang of rustlers.'

'Am I going to have trouble with you, Davis?' asked Bantry quietly. 'If so, you'll have to wait a bit, I haven't had breakfast yet and don't feel like being too polite.'

Davis smiled weakly and shook his head. 'No, I'm over that. Anyway, I want to apologize for my behavior out there on the range the other day. I'd take it as neighborly if you'd join us.'

Bantry glanced at Sullivan, seeing him nod. 'Horace here's told me all about that, Tom. He says he was just going a little crazy. You can understand that, can't you? I mean, having lost everything you've worked for. Now, come on, sit down and tell us about your problems. I hear tell those rustlers got that herd you was rounding up.'

'Yeah, they ran that bunch off, all right. I followed them up into the high country back behind the ranch. Old Leander Harvey owned that up there. Did you know him, Buford?'

Talk around the table halted while Bantry ordered his meal.

'Well, he came into town a few times,' the deputy sheriff answered eventually. 'Someone told me he'd been a trapper or something back before there were any white men in this part of the world. An old-timer, for sure. I didn't know he owned any land, though. What kind of place does he have?'

'He had what he described as a series of high country meadows and a lot of water,' said Bantry, sitting back when the food he'd asked for was placed in front of him. Not speaking until he'd had a bite or two, he went on. 'Pa and I bought it off him not too long ago. He wanted to go down south, said he had a daughter he wanted to visit. We didn't want just anyone to the north of us so we bought it. There's a pass through the mountains and that's what the rustlers were heading for. From the sign I'd say that was the way they ran off at least one other herd before. And, Mr Davis, that could have been how they got your horses out of the basin, too. The trail I was following the day we had our little argument was part of that.'

Davis frowned, looking directly into Tom's eyes. 'I sure feel bad about that.'

Bantry took another bite before responding. 'Don't let it worry you any more. What had happened would have caused anyone to act badly.'

'Good,' Davis sounded relieved. Pulling a turnip watch from his vest pocket he pushed away from the table. 'I'd better get moving. My wife's due to come in on the morning train and I'd better be down there when it arrives. Gentlemen, I'll see you both later?'

'You never did say what happened to the rustlers, Tom,' the lawman said after the other man had gone. 'Did they get away with your herd?'

'No. You ever hear of a man named Garrett? Victor Garrett?'

'Yeah, he's from over Ophir way. Used to work for the mining committee over there. He was hanging around here a short time ago, asking questions about the Stokey gang. I was hoping he'd find them, but I guess he didn't.'

'Yes, he did. Found them and stopped them from making it over the pass with my cows.'

'Now, that's something good to hear He told me he'd been offered a prett good reward for old Hard Luck Hank, dead or alive. You're saying he got him?'

Between bites, Bantry told the deputy sheriff what had happened.

'Well, I never,' Sullivan said finally. 'And you can see all right now?'

'Uh-huh. My eyesight is clear but I have to be easy in how I put my hat on. That scalp wound is still tender.'

'So what now?'

'Go over to talk with Silas is next. Then get some help to go up and bring that herd back down.'

'Well, lots of luck with your banker friend. He's made me feel dirty, delivering those official judgments. You know Davis wasn't the only one. I had to hand out five of them, all signed and legal. But I ain't doing that any more, I don't care how many judges he gets to sign them. It just ain't right. Any more of that and I'll start thinking about giving up the badge and finding something else to do.'

'That certainly don't sound like Silas, ut maybe that's how banks work it now.' Putting a few coins on the table, Bantry stood up. 'Now I feel like I'll make it. Buford, I'll talk with you later.'

No customers were in the bank when Tom Bantry asked to talk with Silas Sidwell. The young clerk standing tall behind the counter shook his head. Bantry had known the two old clerks who used to work in the bank, back when Silas's father was still alive, but he hadn't met either of the two new employees.

'I'm sorry, sir. Mr Sidwell is out at the present time. If you'll leave your name with me I'll let him know you were asking for him.' The youngster was self-important and acting quite proper. Bantry fought to keep from smiling.

'Well, then can you tell me when he'll be back or where I might find him? I've got some bank business to discuss with him.'

'Ah, no. I can't really say where he is but he did tell us he'd be out for at least two days. Is there anything I can do for you?'

Bantry shook his head and frowning left the bank. Now what would he do about the loan coming due? Standing on the boardwalk outside the bank, he thought about it. Glancing up he was surprised to see his father and Billy Horton riding down the street.

'Hey there,' he called out. 'How come you two are in town? I was just thinking about riding out to the ranch.' He waited as the two men reined over and tiredly swung to the ground before going on. 'That herd the rustlers ran off is all safe and the thieves have been dealt with,' young Bantry said quickly, wanting to share the good news. 'I figure it'll take another week or ten days to get them down to the loading pens, but that shouldn't matter. We'll just get an extension on the loan from Silas.'

Asa Bantry caught Horton's eye before looking at his son. 'I have my doubts about getting any extension from Sidwell. Fact is, he's been too busy to be thinking about taking care of any banking business.' Seeing the questioning look on his son's face, the rancher went on. 'He came out to the Flying B last evening, all fired up. Ran us off the place, he did.'

'He what? What do you mean, you got run off.'

'Yep, your banker friend, Sidwell, and some damn fool gunman. They came out to the ranch last night, just about dusk. Had some foreclosure papers, all signed by some judge. Told us we had to vacate. We couldn't argue, he was backed up by that gunslick. There wasn't nothing we could do. Horton here, he wanted to step up to the gunny but I stopped him. Hell's fire, he's still getting over that hit on the head. There was only the three of us on the place when we got run off last night. Lafe, Horton and me. The good banker made us saddle up three horses and ride out.'

27

All Tom Bantry could do was stare at his father with shock written all over his face.

'Wasn't anything we could do, Tom,' Asa Bantry went on. 'What with Lafe's shoulder hurting him, we couldn't ride far. Made camp out along the rocky camping place, you know where I mean? Came on in this morning. Lafe's shoulder was hurting so we dropped him off at Doc Lewis's house to see if he could fix him up.'

'Why, Silas can't do that,' Tom said. 'The loan isn't due for another day or two.' Quickly he tried to remember what day it was. 'Not until the tenth. That's tomorrow. Let's go see what Buford has to say about it.'

Sullivan was sitting in his office, talking with Horace Davis and a stranger.

'This is Carl Reavis,' the deputy sheriff introduced the newcomer. 'Old Horace here said you suggested that he go talk with someone down at the capital, Tom, you remember?'

Young Bantry shook his head. 'Nope, I might have said anything, having a bunch pointing their weapons at me.'

'Ah, Bantry, I told you how bad I feel about that.'

Sullivan cut in. 'That don't matter anymore, let it go. Reavis here is a state marshal. Seems the governor had been hearing some complaints about one of the judges he'd appointed for this county. When Horace explained how he'd lost his ranch, the governor called in Reavis and sent him up here to find out what's been happening.'

'This gentleman's story isn't the first one we heard about,' said the marshal.

Anyone riding into Ferris Corners the first time would know Buford Sullivan represented the law; his badge was big, shiny and was pinned just above the man's shirt pocket. There was

271

no such sign that this man, Reavis, was with the law. Fact is, Bantry thought, looking at his low-heeled shoes and black wool suit, he looked more like a lawyer or even a banker. The only indication that this was not someone to fool with was his hard, square-jawed, unsmiling face and the revolver hanging butt down in a shoulder holster.

'For some time the governor has been getting letters from businessmen up in La Platte, complaining about how Judge Welch was letting convicted men off with a slap on the back. The worst case was giving a man who'd been convicted of holding up a hardware store a fifty dollar fine. It's hard, though, to do anything about such things. But now we might have our chance.'

'And what exactly would that mean to us, Mister Marshal?' Asa Bantry asked. 'Buford, we came in to tell you that Sidwell ran us off the Flying B last evening. He had some young gunslinger siding him and there weren't nothing we could do. Now you got the state involved, what's going to happen?'

'Damn,' Sullivan cursed, 'you see, Marshal, this is the sorta thing that's been going on for the past few months. I've had to go out to at least five ranches, delivering foreclosure notices all signed by that judge up at the county seat. Asa, I had one here with your name on it. When Sidwell brought it in I told him to hold off on it. I had had enough. Told him to get some other lawman to do his dirty work. He got all huffy and stormed out.'

'Well, gentlemen, there's not much I can do until I hear from the state's attorneys. I came ahead while they were researching the note and foreclosure notice that Mr Davis here had given us. That might be enough to overturn those foreclosures, but what we really want is evidence of complicity between Judge Welch and Sidwell.'

Tom Bantry, standing next to the office door, frowned. 'Are you saying we got to wait?'

'At least until I hear from the capital. I'm expecting a telegram at any time.'

★   ★   ★

Tom Bantry didn't like it, but both his father and Buford said they'd go along with it. The Ferris Corners lawman invited Tom over to see how Cora Lee was doing while they waited.

'No, I'd like to but I think I'll stay with Pa and Horton. There're a few things we have to talk about.'

Sullivan, leaving the state marshal to his own ends, walked over to his fiancée's place for the mid-day meal. Their plans were to get married shortly before Christmas but with Mattie's two house guests, he was starting to worry about that happening. He hadn't brought it up knowing how Mattie would react. What else could she do, kick them out? And just where would they go? He could already hear in his mind the questions she'd ask. No, better just to let things work themselves out.

'Hey,' he called, sticking his head into Mattie's front door, 'anybody home?'

'Yes, we're back here, Buford, in the kitchen.'

The two young women were always busy, it seemed, either baking or sewing or cleaning.

'Come on back,' Mattie called. 'I suppose you've come by to see if the coffee is fresh brewed?'

Mattie and Cora were sitting at the big table, steaming cups sitting in saucers in front of them. Cora stared into her cup while Mattie rose from her chair to go over to the big wood stove to get Buford a cup of coffee.

'We've just been sitting here talking,' Mattie said, 'and the morning's got away from us,' she laughed. 'Neither of us watched the time. I guess I'd better see about something for lunch. Cora, why don't you tell Buford what we've been getting done today?'

Buford waited a moment but Cora didn't even look up. Damn, she still would talk only when there was no man around. He didn't understand that at all.

'Well, I guess I've got some news I can share with you two. Tom Bantry and his pa came into the office a bit ago. Tom said he'd chased down the rustlers what stole his herd, you know, the one he was selling to pay off a loan at the bank? Well, it seems our local banker couldn't wait for that to happen, Asa Bantry said young Sidwell and a gunslick chased him and old Lafe off the place last night. Taking it over, he said, waving another one of them foreclosure documents around.'

Hearing the news, Mattie stopped what she was doing to stare at Buford.

'You mean Mr Sidwell didn't wait for you to deliver the papers?'

'No. He brought them in to me but I told him I wouldn't take anymore of those kinds of things to anyone. And there's more. A state marshal has come into town. He's waiting for some kind of confirmation that all those fore-closures weren't legal. That could mean trouble for Sidwell, I reckon.'

'So that means the Bantrys won't lose their ranch?'

'Well,' Buford sat back, staring at his hands folded on the table, 'I don't know about that. It does seem strange, though, that Sidwell would jump the gun. I thought that the Bantry note wasn't due until tomorrow. Man, that Sidwell is certainly asking for trouble.'

'Where's Tom's herd? Can he get it sold in time to pay off that note?'

'Now, that's the bad news. The rustlers ran those critters somewhere up into the high country. Tom said he figured it'd take another week or so to get them down to the pens.' He sipped his coffee before going on. 'Guess it'll be up to that marshal and the law to sort it all out. Davis might be getting his place back, from what he was told. But I dunno. It all sounds like trouble, to me. I just don't know exactly who for.'

Cora's head had come up at the mention of Tom Bantry but neither

Buford or Mattie had noticed. As Mattie was putting a plate of sliced ham and a loaf of bread on the table, Cora got up and went out of the room.

'I hope I didn't disturb her,' Buford said, reaching for the bread knife.

'I can't see why. You go ahead and eat; I'll go see what the matter is.'

Buford had finished a second sandwich before both women returned. Mattie came back in to the kitchen with a big smile.

'Buford, did you say that the Bantry bank loan isn't due until tomorrow?'

'Well, that's what I heard. Leastways that's what I seem to recall. Why?'

Mattie ignored the question. 'And did you happen to hear just how much that loan was for?'

'Naw, nobody ever said anything like that. Probably wasn't big, considering they were going to pay it off with the sale of a hundred head or so.'

'Could you guess an amount?'

'Hmmm, well, let's see. This time of year isn't the usual time for a cattle buyer to be dickering much. But then there's not a lot of cattle heading for market either.' He sat back, thinking. 'Well, it's damn hard to say, but if the price of beef was half of that paid out in the spring, I'd think they'd bring in maybe twenty-five dollars a head. Figure to use the herd to clear the note, it'd likely be in the $2,500 to $3,000 range. Now why these questions?'

'Buford,' Mattie's smile was huge. 'Cora thinks she's got a way to help the Bantrys out. Come on, get your hat, let's go over to town.'

28

'What are we doing?' Buford Sullivan whispered, holding the front door to the bank for Cora and Mattie.

'Just watch, Buford.'

Mattie stepped up to the window. Standing on the other side with a welcoming smile, a youngish man waited, his coal-black hair slicked down against his head all shiny with some kind of pomade.

'Good morning, ladies and Sheriff. How can we help you today?'

'We'd like to see Mr Sidwell,' Mattie requested softly. Sullivan frowned, wondering if Mattie hadn't heard him tell how the banker had chased everyone out of the Flying B ranch.

'I'm sorry, he is out of the bank and expects to be gone for the next few days. Maybe one of us can help you,' he nodded to another man standing next

280

to a desk toward the back.

'Well, you see, we're here to make a payment on a bank loan,' Mattie went on, further mystifying the deputy sheriff.

'Oh, yes, Scott will be happy to take care of you,' the first man said, then raising his voice a little called to the man in back. 'Scott, Miss Andrews wishes to speak with you. Go right back, m'am,' he motioned, his smile never leaving his face.

'First off, would you be so kind as to weigh out this?' Still frowning, Sullivan watched as his fiancée dropped four small leather pouches on the desk. When the bank clerk emptied one into the palm of his hand, Sullivan nearly choked when he saw the gold nuggets, all about the same size.

'Where — ?' was all he could get out before Mattie shushed him.

'We'll wait,' she said, taking Sullivan by the arm and leading him a few steps back while the clerk proceeded to bring out a set of balance scales. Cora stood quietly to one side, watching every move the bank clerk made.

'What the hell's going on, Mattie?' Sullivan whispered, also watching the clerk.

'Cora wanted to help the Bantrys. She told me that Tom Bantry had saved her and Bobby from that Rufus Earle and she couldn't let anyone take away his ranch. So, we're here to pay off the loan. Didn't you say the note wasn't due until tomorrow?'

'Yeah, but old Sidwell's already gone out there and taken over.'

'Well, then he can just come back here, can't he?'

'But where'd Cora get that much gold?'

Mattie sighed. 'Cora hid it. She said when her mother died her pa took to drinking and gambling. She tried to get her father to sober up but he seemed to have lost his mind. Thinking she'd better do something to protect her brother and herself, she sewed those little bags of gold nuggets in the bottom of her heavy wool coat.'

'She stole the gold?'

'No, Buford,' she said exasperatedly. 'It was gold nuggets from the mine her father owned. She took them before he lost it in a poker game. She hoped once her pa hit bottom, he'd settle down and then with that gold they could start over. But, well, it didn't work out that way. She hasn't explained everything to me, but she is sure her pa's dead.'

'And now she's ready to give it all to the Bantrys.' said Sullivan in wonder.

'Oh, I think it'll work out. Haven't you seen the way Tom looks at her? C'mon, that clerk is finished.'

★ ★ ★

Cora still wouldn't speak to the deputy sheriff but once out of the bank, she handed the loan paper marked 'Paid' to him.

Mattie explained for her. 'We thought it would be best if you gave this to Tom. He might not understand if it came straight out from either of us.'

Buford Sullivan, still shaking his head in awe, could only nod in agreement. Both Tom and Asa were, he thought, over at the saloon. That would be good. After this little bit of business, he felt a strong need for a drink.

Signaling to Fat Henry for a drink, Sullivan just handed the slip of paper to the elder Bantry.

'What's this,' Asa Bantry asked, taking his spectacles from a shirt pocket and carefully fitting each end of the wire frame over his ears in turn.

'What is it, Pa?' asked Tom, not really showing much interest.

Standing on the other side of Tom and his father, Marshal Carl Reavis, holding a half-empty beer mug, craned his head around to watch.

'I dunno, son,' said Asa looking at the deputy sheriff as the lawman sipped his drink and tried to look innocent. 'Buford, is this some kind of joke?'

'Nope. It's for real and I'd say it might make things a little difficult for our town banker.'

Handing the note to Tom, Asa looked back at Sullivan for an explanation.

'Look, all I can tell you is that Cora Lee had some gold hidden away. She dug it out and went down to the bank and paid off that note. The wheres and whys of it all you'll have to take up with her. Now, what're you gonna do about that piece of paper you got in your hand, Tom?'

'Yeah,' the young Bantry said slowly, 'I guess something will have to be done, won't it.'

Sullivan nodded. 'For certain there ain't nothing I can do, and our good friend from the governor's office is still waiting for some kind of information. To top it off, here's your friend.'

'Hey, there, boss,' Billy Horton had been sitting at one of the tables talking with friends but came over to hear the last part. 'I guess if I'm still riding for the brand, I'd better go along with you, if'n you're heading back out to the ranch, that is.'

'Billy, I'd be pleased to have you along,' Tom responded, a big smile breaking out. Turning to his father, he chuckled. 'Pa, you might want to do some shopping while you're in town. I seem to recall Lafe complaining that he'd had to empty out the larder for those hungry cowboys during that round-up. Buford, Marshal, talk to you another time.'

★   ★   ★

Not wanting to ride in after dark, Tom and Horton rode out a piece from town, breaking the ride at about the same place his pa had done when coming into town. Lying in his bedroll after a last cup of coffee, Tom stared up at the stars, trying to plan for the next morning. All he could think of was Cora and that gold.

Buford hadn't bothered to explain any further than to say the gold did come from her pa's mine, back before he lost it all gambling. Now why, he wondered, would she take it to the bank to pay off the Flying B's loan?

He figured from what that man, Garrett had said, he kinda understood the reason she wasn't talking. At least not to men. Basically being sold by her father to pay a gambling debt would bother any woman. To make it worse, who knew how badly she'd been treated by that fool Rufus Earle? And then to spend her money like that. It didn't make sense.

The two men were up with the sun and after boiling up a fresh pot of coffee, they spent some time checking the loads in their six-guns.

'That gunslick you said came in with Silas,' asked Bantry as he ran a rag through his Colt's barrel, 'did you know him?'

'Well, no. I can't say I heard him say anything. But you know, I seem to think maybe I saw him once before. Back there when the rustlers hit us and ran off the herd, I was knocked clean outa the saddle. Them damn fools shot my horse out from under me and then before I could get my six-gun to working, one of them came up and shot me. Just sat his horse and laughed and shot me. I couldn't clearly see him, what with the sun behind his head and all. But there was something about that gunman siding the banker that reminded me of that rustler.'

'I wonder,' Tom said, remembering what Garrett had said about his chasing the others off over the pass after killing Stokey. One of them didn't go that way, the one that had put the bullet against his own head. 'I wonder if that couldn't have been Jesse Earle backing up Silas's play.'

'I dunno. Don't ever recall meeting any of the Earle brothers. Heard you had a run in with them, but that's about all.'

'Yeah. Well it wouldn't surprise me any. Come on, let's get this show on the road.'

The wagon road ran as straight as a catch rope from the front gate up to the ranch buildings. Anyone coming to visit could be seen at least two miles away. Before getting that close, Tom and Horton angled off, staying behind a low ridge. The ridge ran behind the barn and other outbuildings before joining up with a higher hill. Turning just before reaching a huge old oak tree, Tom slowly rode up until he could look over the top of the ridge and stopped.

'Here's what I thought we could do,' he said as Horton reined in next to his horse. 'We take it easy and drop down, keeping the barn between us and the main house. If we leave the horses tied to a corral rail, we should be able to get around the barn and into the back door of the house without being seen. That's where I figure they'll be, in the house. I don't know what'll happen then, but we'll have surprise on our side.'

Horton only nodded, unconsciously settling his handgun in its holster.

Stepping carefully and taking their time, with Tom in the lead, they stopped at the far corner of the barn.

The only movement was from a half-dozen chickens picking and scratching in the twenty feet or so of yard between the barn and the back of the house. Tom could hear the hens clucking as they scratched the dirt.

'That's it,' Tom said, keeping his voice down. 'I'll go first and you kinda stay back. If I can make it unseen I'll wait before opening the back door and you come over.'

'Do we shoot 'em if we can?'

Tom hesitated. 'I'd rather not. If they want to make it difficult, then don't hang back. What I'd really like to do, though, is talk with Sidwell a bit. But we can't take any chances. Especially if that's Jesse Earle with him. Earle knows I killed his brothers and has already done his damnedest to pay me back. Watch him close.'

'All right. I'll cover you.'

Giving the rest of the yard a quick glance, Tom stepped out and walked slowly, not wanting to scare the hens into a noisy scamper. He was past the clucking hens when he heard someone behind him.

'Well, looky here.'

Tom stopped, swinging around, half-drawing his Colt before freezing, looking down the barrel of a rifle, the gun held by a smirking Jesse Earle.

29

Grinning from ear to ear, Earle went on, enjoying the opportunity to crow. 'You know, that banker feller was right. He figured you'd be coming around this morning and here you are. Having me sit out in the barn, just in case, was a right smart move, don't ya think?'

'What you got there, Earle,' Tom heard Silas Sidwell call from the front of the house. Turning a little so he could keep Earle in sight, Tom watched Silas walk out into the yard, still wearing his usual dark wool suit as if going to his bank. His coat was unbuttoned. Leather straps crossed his chest, holding a shoulder holster tight under his left armpit.

'Well, now isn't this nice,' Sidwell said, his voice sounding thin. 'I really didn't expect that excuse for a sheriff the town hired to show up. Knowing you as I do, Tom, I knew it'd be you that came out. And I'm glad you did. There's a few things I'd like to tell you before, well, before I let young Earle here do what he wants so badly.'

Tom couldn't believe it. Silas was actually chuckling.

Ignoring Earle, Tom stared at Silas, trying to figure out what was causing him to act this way. The pair had been friends since school days. Now his friend was acting like someone that'd been chewing on loco weed. Scowling with his lack of understanding he didn't see Horton step away from the corner of the barn.

Earle was glaring at Bantry and didn't see the cowboy stop a few yards to the side.

'Hey,' Horton said softly, his Colt held at his side.

'What — ?' Earle twisted toward the voice, bringing his rifle around. Horton shot him.

Glancing quickly back at Silas, Tom drew his own revolver. 'Go ahead, Sil·

Finish pulling that gun of yours and I'll shoot you where you stand.'

The banker stood for a moment as if thinking about it, then pushed the weapon snugly back in its holster.

'Well, there is no for any need of that, Tom. Before you do anything unwarranted, think about it. What will a jury say if you kill the banker you'd lost your ranch to? Murder is a hanging offence, you know, and that's what it'd be. No, old friend, I suggest you and your friend there just get back on your horses and ride out. Oh, and take that body with you. One just can't leave things like that lying around. It doesn't look good.'

Tom stood, surprised. This was the man he thought he knew and he was actually laughing. Shaking his head, Tom walked over and pulled the revolver from Silas's shoulder holster.

'No reason to take that, Tom. I'm not about to use it on you. I don't have to. The law is on my side, you know.'

'Nope, I don't know. Silas, what

happened to you? Lately you've been acting like a crazy man, foreclosing on all the ranches in the basin. I purely don't understand it.'

'Ah, Tom. You see, that's been your problem. You always were satisfied with being a working hand. That's all you ever wanted, to be a good little rancher. Well, that was not enough for me, I wanted more. All those times when you came riding in, sitting so tall and proud in the saddle, looking down at me because I was a townie. Even though all you ranchers couldn't get along without my father's money, his loans, yes, his bank, you still thought yourself better than him. He couldn't see it but I could. Oh, yes. We had the money your kind needed but because we wore clean clothes and polished shoes we were never considered one with you. No, we could discuss things like good music and art while all you cowboys knew about was cattle. Even in school I knew you were laughing at me. Well, now who's laughing, huh?'

'What are you talking about? I never looked down on you or anyone.'

Ignoring Tom's words Sidwell pulled his shoulders back and, if anything, stood a little taller. 'And now, even now, when you need money, who do you go to? Me! My bank. But I'm not good enough that you'll tell me what the money's for. Oh, no. I'm merely a small-town banker. I wouldn't understand what a rancher would need extra cash for. Well, now I'm the rancher. Now people will listen to me when I speak. Not only do I control the bank, I own title to half a dozen ranches. Hear that, Tom? Not one measly little spread like this, half a dozen.'

Shaking his head, Tom pulled the bank note from his pocket. 'No, Silas, I hate to bust your dream but you don't own the Flying B.'

'You still think you'll get your herd to the loading pens in time to pay off that note? Ha! Stokey and his boys would have already sold those beeves and likely have spent the money on some floozies if it hadn't been for some bad luck. But what do I care? Your cattle are too far away to make it to the loading pens. No cattle to ship, no money to pay that debt. Too bad. Then there's that fool Earle coming in with some story about you being killed. Can you believe it? He even claimed Stokey and his gang had been run off. Well, when I saw you just now I knew he'd been lying. He always was a damn fool.'

'This time,' Tom holding out the paper, 'that foolish youngster was telling the truth. I wasn't killed, the herd is safe and Stokey is dead. I saw him myself, tied over his saddle.'

Sidwell paused, 'Well, even if that's true, you can't get that herd to market in time to pay off that loan I made you. This is my property and I'll thank you to take your friend and ride off of it.'

'Again you messed up. Silas, what made you think you could chase my pa and old Lafe off the place? The note isn't due until tomorrow,' thinking a bit, Tom had to smile, 'or rather today.

That note wasn't due when you and Earle there came in and scared two old men. Why?'

'That fool of a deputy sheriff wouldn't do it. I had the foreclosure papers all signed and he wouldn't bring them out. So I did it myself. Yes, maybe I was a day or two early, but I'd been told you were dead. I didn't think it would matter and it made me feel good. But it doesn't matter, does it. Today is the day and the herd is still up in the high country.' He stopped to laugh. 'Oh, I get it, you're going to ask for an extension. Not a chance. This is my ranch now.'

'Take a look at this, will you? The loan payment was made yesterday. Your judge signed those foreclosure papers for no reason. The loan has been paid.'

'What?' Grabbing the paper, he quickly scanned it, seeing the red stamp 'paid' marked across the center. 'Who did this? It can't be.'

'That signature is from one of your bank clerks.'

'They had no right to sign anything. This isn't worth beans.'

'Oh, yes, I think it is. The money for the loan was paid into your bank and the note marked paid. Now, I'd be saddling up and riding for town, was I you. Maybe you can get to the bottom of things there. But right now, we've got a would-be bad man to bury.'

30

Tom hadn't planned on riding back into town but after thinking about it, decided it would be better to take Earle's body to the undertaker.

'Just planting him out behind the barn doesn't seem right,' he explained to Horton.

Wrapping the body in a sheet of canvas, he placed it in the back of a ranch wagon and headed toward Ferris Corners. Billy Horton thought he'd better go along in case Deputy Sheriff Sullivan or that state marshal had any questions.

'It don't bother me none, shooting that jasper,' he told Tom, 'he was fixing to do me in. Anyway, I still think he was part of that gang of rustlers. No sir, having the last of the Earle brothers in the ground shouldn't upset anybody.'

Tom Bantry half expected to meet up

with his pa and Lafe on the ride in but didn't. Wanting to get rid of the dead man, his first stop was at the deputy sheriff's office.

'I've been expecting you boys,' Sullivan said, lifting a corner of the canvas to look at Earle's still pale face. 'Sidwell came busting in a couple hours ago, all foam and froth. Left his horse at the hitch rack and stormed into the bank. We could hear him ranting and raving clear out on the street.' The law man chuckled. 'It was kinda funny, except I don't think those two clerks of his was thinking so. They're both over to the hotel, packing their bags. Guess Sidwell thinks he can run the bank by hisself. Well, I'll take this over to the undertaker. Mayor Yelton won't like it when I tell him the city'll have to pay for the funeral. You boys going over to the Mex's for coffee? I think that's where your pa was headed, Tom.'

Bantry nodded and said he'd buy the coffee after Sullivan came back from the undertaker's.

Finding Lafe sitting next to his pa made Tom feel better. 'I was wondering what had happened to you, Lafe,' he said, pulling out a chair. 'Thought Billy here and I would have to go up by ourselves to bring those cows back down.'

'You leave Lafe alone, Tom,' Asa Bantry ordered. 'Doc Lewis said he shouldn't be doing anything for a while to let that wound heal up right. Now, tell us what happened. All we saw was your friend Silas come storming into town.'

Quickly Tom told about the shooting of Jesse Earle and having run Sidwell off the Flying B.

'I don't know what went wrong with Silas, but something certainly changed. He's not the man I called friend, that's for sure.'

Asa nodded, 'Well, I don't think it'll matter much longer. That state marshal, Reavis, he got his telegram. Seems the judge that's been signing all those foreclosure notices was getting paid off for each one. Some kind of shady deal between Sidwell and him. I don't understand it, but it appears that the bank's doors will be closed while Sidwell goes down to the capital to answer a whole passel of charges.'

Buford Sullivan came in just in time to hear the last of that statement.

'Well, that's it for the Earle family. Jesse'll be buried and nobody'll remember which grave is his by this time next year without a headstone. You know, it's almost too bad Jesse Earle's dead,' he continued thoughtfully. 'He'd be about the only one who could tell us what part Silas played with all that rustling that's been going on. He had to have been behind it but nobody'd ever be able to prove it now.'

Heads around the table nodded.

'I said about the same thing to the state marshal,' Sullivan continued, 'and he assured me that wouldn't matter. The governor's office has prepared enough charges against Sidwell and the judge to put them in the state prisor until both are old men. Of course,' he mused almost to himself, 'there's a bunch of ranchers getting their property back who would've liked to have a hand in stringing up that whole bunch of rustlers, with Sidwell being the first.'

Again everybody nodded in agreement.

'And that,' said the elder Bantry after a moment, 'brings us around to the question of what will we do about Cora? She really saved the day, you know. Tom, do you think she'll let us return her money once we sell that herd?'

Sullivan cut in before Tom could speak.

'I think, if'n it was me, I'd go have a little talk with her before getting too carried away with trying to pay her back.' Holding up a hand, he went on, 'I'm not speaking for her, mind you. She certainly don't say much, at least not to me, but I figure she's got a mind of her own. I'm just thinking of myself, here.'

Everybody waited, expecting him to go on. Frowning and with a shake of his head, the deputy sheriff explained. 'Now, look boys, you all know me'n Mattie want to get married, don't you? Well, we plan to live there in Mattie's house. It's a lot bigger than that little cabin I been living in. Anyway it ain't that there's not enough room for Cora and her little brother, but, well, we'd kinda like to have the place to ourselves.'

'So, what are you suggesting, Buford?' asked Lafe who happened to have a big smile on his face.

'Well, she does own a piece of the Flying B now, doesn't she? And if I remember rightly, there are a couple bedrooms in the main house out there going empty. Now, if'n Tom here were to take up residence in the bunk house, then nobody'd talk and everybody'd be happy. And Tom,' for the first time Sullivan looked directly at the other man, 'little Bobby was telling me how you'd promised to take him fishing. Ain't that so?'

Tom was caught. Glancing first at his pa then at the town's lawman, he grimaced.

'I don't know if that'd work out, Buford. I mean, yeah, she's got some money coming and she'll get it soon as that herd's sold, but,' shaking his head side to side, he hesitated. 'I mean, here in town she's got Mattie to talk to. From what I know about it, she won't talk when there's any man around and that's all that'll be out at the ranch — men.'

Buford Sullivan smiled 'You know, that's an interesting thing. We was sitting around the table having supper last night, Mattie, Cora and me, talking about the Flying B and the banker and such, when I saw how Cora was listening. Now usually she don't look up at me when I'm talking. She'll look at Mattie and even smile at her at times, but never at me. Always keeping her head down, you know. Well, this time she's not only looking at me while was telling them about what Marshal

Reavis had been told in his telegram, she was smiling. Tom, I think maybe someone ought to talk to her a little. See what she's thinking. All I know is she's got to find a place for her and her brother, a safe place. And much as I like them two, that place ain't here in town.'

For a long few minutes none of the men spoke.

Eventually, Asa Bantry stood up. 'Uh-huh. It is a real problem, isn't it? Well, Lafe, Horton, let's go get those supplies we're going to need and head out toward the ranch. There's a lot of work to get done before winter sets in. Tom, you know, that boy, Bobby. He's about the right age to be started teaching how to work on a ranch, don't you think?'

After all the others had gone, leaving Buford and Tom alone, neither man said anything, just sat quietly sipping at their coffee. Emptying his cup, Tom pushed away from the table.

'You think sooner or later she'll talk to me?' he asked the other man.

'Only one way to find out, I reckon. Go ask her.'

Nodding and giving the deputy sheriff a little wave, the cowboy turned and walked out.

THE END

We do hope that you have enjoyed reading this large print book.

Did you know that all of our titles are available for purchase?

We publish a wide range of high quality large print books including:
Romances, Mysteries, Classics
General Fiction
Non Fiction and Westerns

Special interest titles available in large print are:
The Little Oxford Dictionary
Music Book, Song Book
Hymn Book, Service Book

Also available from us courtesy of Oxford University Press:
Young Readers' Dictionary
(large print edition)
Young Readers' Thesaurus
(large print edition)

For further information or a free brochure, please contact us at:
Ulverscroft Large Print Books Ltd.,
The Green, Bradgate Road, Anstey,
Leicester, LE7 7FU, England.
Tel: (00 44) **0116 236 4325**
Fax: (00 44) **0116 234 0205**

BY THE GUN THEY DIED

Matt James

With seven killers camped on his trail, big Blaze Morgan rides south into Weeping Woman Valley. With his superior gun skills and horseman-ship, Morgan expects that he will soon shake off his pursuers. But it's a dark and a stormy night and when he's violently thrown from his horse he finds that he will be lucky to survive the next twenty-four hours . . . Can he ever hope to overcome the obstacles in his way?

GONE TO TEXAS

J. D. Ryder

Andy and Cletus, wounded late in the Civil War, flee the battlefield and head for home . . . but Yankee carpetbaggers have taken over. Andy's family has been evicted from their ranch, so he turns to what he learned in the war: how to kill. The enemies now are Yankee politicians who came south to loot and plunder. When 'Wanted' posters circulate, however, the two friends join a cattle drive going to Texas, but the brutal past finally catches up with them.

RANSOM

Owen G. Irons

In Crater, Arizona, Amos Fillmore is the town's banker. His life is shattered when a gang led by the notorious gunman, Earl Weathers, kidnaps his daughter, Anita. Duplicity and violence rage while Anita languishes in a cave deep into the hills of the desert wilderness. Her safety is compromised by greed — that of the kidnappers and those tasked with upholding justice. It's only when the territory's top gun, Laredo, arrives that Anita and her ransom can ever be recovered.

PACKING IRON

Steve Hayes

Rebellious teenager Raven Bjorkman and her widowed mother, Ingrid, save the life of Gabriel Moonlight, an outlaw dying from gunshot wounds. They learn that he was shot by his enemy's son, Stadtlander, a ruthless rancher. Gabriel rides off, leaving Raven and Ingrid caring deeply for him. Then, when they move to Old Calico in California, they are unexpectedly reunited with Gabriel who finds himself in a perilous situation where only his gun-skills will save the day.

RAIDERS OF THE MISSION SAN JUAN

Scott Connor

On the trail of the Shannon gang, Marshal Lincoln Hawk learns that they have already been killed. Believing that the dead outlaws have been incorrectly identified he continues on the owlhoot trail. He finds the gang still very much alive at the Mission San Juan, preparing to claim a stash of Mexican gold. Whilst the gang fiercely protect their alibi, no help is forthcoming from the peaceful mission padres. As Lincoln confronts an army of gun-toting raiders can he hold his own?